DAVIDE

the
tooth
fairy

ISBN: 978-1-7923-8066-2

Cover design & interior formatting:
Mark Thomas / Coverness.com

This book is for Sandy.
She truly believed this day would come,
way more than I did.

The oldest and strongest emotion of mankind is fear,
And the oldest and strongest kind of fear is the fear of
the unknown.

H.P. Lovecraft

And the most terrifying question of all may be just how
much horror the human mind can stand and still maintain
a wakeful, staring, unrelenting sanity.

Stephen King

And when you gaze long into the abyss,
the abyss gazes long into you.

Frederich Nietzche

CHAPTER ONE:

THE BLUR AND THE PAIN

1

July 4, 2018

It was dark when he regained consciousness. The pain came only after—but still earlier than any other perception or memory. Every single part of his body—the ones he was able to feel—ached in different measures. The pain was so scattered that he wasn't sure what hurt the most. Not even the worst hangover of his life could compare to whatever his body was experiencing now.

He opened his eyes. His sight seemed a little better this time. Confused lines started to come back in place on the edges of the objects in front of him.

Will the world eventually stop spinning? He wondered, as he closed his eyes again and groaned. A ragged exhale came out of his lungs. He forced himself to give it another try, so he glimpsed through the room he was in. Shadows and objects were taking shape, dancing out of focus right in front of him in a kaleidoscopic party. His mouth was dry and filled with a metallic taste. *Coins*, he thought. *My mouth tastes like a bunch of quarters*. His head was a throbbing bass drum. He could feel his heartbeat in the nape of his neck, fast and deep. His panting echoed from the inside; he could feel it in his ears. The groans were loud in his head. It was like listening to the world from a stethoscope.

He tried to move but he couldn't. He tried to raise his right hand, but he couldn't—nor could he raise his left hand or move his legs. Eventually, he realized that he was lying in a dental chair. His arms were secured to the armrests with duct tape; his legs were taped together and to the chair's extension. It felt like being on a recliner—just a less comfortable one, surrounded by odd tools. Between his body and the chair was a thin layer that he guessed was cellophane; when he tried to rock his body on the chair, it stuck to his sweaty back. He was shirtless and barefoot. The only thing he wore was a pair of jeans.

What the hell?

The task of raising his head required all his effort and determination. He took a deep breath and swayed his neck more violently than he had meant to. Like all mistakes, it was too late when he judged it to be so. The world blurred more, and the room started spinning in front of him at worrying speed. He closed his eyes again. When even the darkness of his eyelids started spinning, he stuck his head out and threw up on his lap. Judging from the consistency of the hot and acidic fluid spread on his legs, he hadn't ingested anything solid in a while.

With no reason, he started laughing, finally confirming the thought that crept in the back of his mind. Yes, he was high as shit. He laughed harder, in an extraneous stirring that he couldn't control. He couldn't tell whether he had been in the chair for two minutes, two hours, or two days. The only thing he had a perception of was the spinning. The hysterical laughter coming out from his mouth didn't sound like anything belonging to him. Then the memories started to come back forcefully. He had rejected them all at first. There was too much going on already. But they could not be pushed away forever. He could snooze them, but they would come back relentlessly. And indeed, they came now like a wind, wiping all doubts away.

In the storm of his thoughts, he remembered all at once. Something triggered the chain reaction. It felt like turning the master switch on in a warehouse filled with darkness. He could almost hear the buzzing sound of neon lights turning on in sequence, revealing bits of information. With every row of lights switching on, he felt a wave of discomfort and desperation growing. He observed it rising inside with raging dread. He laughed again, hard and against his will. It was just as uncontrollable as the spinning. He was on a nightmarish merry-go-round where everything was amplified. He forced himself to escape from the dreadful pictures that were accumulating in the darkness and opened his eyes.

He knew exactly where he was. He had been here before,

and not very long ago. The room he was in was large and had a low ceiling. It was divided into two sections, with two different floors. One was covered in square, green tiles. The other was dark, uniform material that looked like slate. An unfinished wooden staircase loomed on the other side of the room. The narrow, rectangular windows near the top of the walls confirmed his latest memories. He was in a basement. The light passing through the windows was still strong and spotlighted his surroundings. The place was a marvel of cleanliness and, aside from the vomit, smelled of bleach and disinfectant. Beneath the windows, a row of steel cabinets and drawers rested against the wall. On the counter were objects, shapes he couldn't quite put in focus yet.

He turned his head, and this time he was able to control the impulse to retch better than he had before. He slowly opened his eyes again and gently turned his head to the left, discovering a dark corner of the room. There were no windows on that side, and the sunbeams filtering from the others could not reach that far. There was a coat rack standing on the floor in the farthest corner. The shadows on the wall made it look like a tall and skinny creature, stretching its long arms in an impossible attempt to reach the light.

His mind went back to the main problem. He had already lay on that chair, just not tied up, not as a prisoner. And that was the moment when he finally realized he was a prisoner indeed.

How fucking ironic, he considered, sitting on the same

chair where he had once believed the pain would finally cease. He focused on the chair with its four branches, one at the top and one at the bottom of each side; every branch had several extensions. The bottom arm on his left carried a blood-stained oval sink, the kind where people rinse and spit. It wasn't made of white plastic, like the one at the dentist's office he had been to in the past; this one looked like steel, suggesting that it belonged to a dentist from another time. As the pain became clearer and more localized, he checked his gums with the tip of his tongue. The ferrous taste became stronger, mixed with an unpleasant sweetness, as if something was rotting in his mouth. His tongue found a hole in his upper left arch and felt something was wrong, not in place.

He turned his head to the other side, glancing at another branch of the chair. It was a mirror, and somehow, he was certain it had been left there so he could use it. It was there for him to see. He shivered as a wave of terror crested inside his chest. The mirror was pointed way too far to the left to reflect anything that was of use to him. He used all his strength to create a gap between his palms and the chair, but the effort was futile. Either the duct tape was way stronger than he would have expected, or he was much weaker than usual. His arms didn't move an inch. As a sense of impotence pervaded, he let himself weep. The sound echoed in the room as the sunbeams, flooding from the windows, became weaker on the walls. He screamed in a desperate outburst, swaying in vain. His mind traveled all the way back to when he was nine, reading about

Harry Houdini. He wished he had learned something from all those illusion books.

He sensed something underneath the pointer finger of his right hand. A rounded and knurled surface brushed the numb fingertip. He tried to push it, but his finger slipped—and he saw one of the chair's arms wobbling. He realized it was a knob. He played with it, rolling it back and forth, and realized with some disappointment that the knob could not move the arm with the mirror. The only arm of the chair that it did activate was one bearing a tiny metallic tool with the shape of a hook. The mechanism squeaked loudly in the deep silence of the room, where the only noise he'd heard so far had been his own panting.

Oh, come on, for fuck's sake, he thought as his hopes began to abandon him. He extended all his fingers, looking for something else. His fists hadn't been clenched when he was tied to the chair, but open on the armrests, with the tape wrapping the wrists and palms, so that the thumbs could move freely.

She wants me to be able to see myself in the mirror, he realized—and another sudden wave of fear assaulted him.

He moved both his thumbs in circles, trying to cover as much area as he could.

He found a switch on the right side. It seemed to have three positions: forward, center, and backward. He moved it back and forth, but nothing happened. It took him a bit to understand the switch was a selector, to move different tools with the knob he had found before. He shifted it all the way backward and then tried the knob. Finally, the mirror began to move toward him.

As the contours of his features became visible in the reflection in the mirror, he knew right away that the troubles he had put himself in were far worse than he could have ever imagined. His face was a triumph of swellings and clotted blood nuances on the ghastly background of his skin. His right eye socket was a dark purple circle—as if he had been punched, hard. The swollen jaws made him look like a grotesque caricature of himself. He forced himself to smile in front of the mirror. When he did so, he closed his eyes instinctively. He wanted to scream, but no sounds came out of his mouth.

With a violent spasm, he vomited again on his lap. He took a deep breath before giving another glance at the mirror, afraid of what was expecting him beyond the clamped lips. On the lower arch, the two central incisors were bandaged with tiny cotton capsules, each of which showed a clotted red area on the top.

And slowly, almost like the brain had been waiting for him to see before pulling the trigger, the pain was back. Not entirely back—but he could feel it pulsating to the same beat as the headache throbbing in his temples. He opened his mouth and looked back in the mirror, then gently patted the cotton capsules with his tongue, searching for the hard edges of his teeth with no success. His teeth were gone—and not the ones that were supposed to go. When he tried to apply more pressure, an electric impulse of pure pain blasted through his gums, reaching back into his head, straight to the brain.

He screamed.

Oh fuck...fuck...fuck.

He gasped, avidly searching for oxygen in the still and hot air of the room. The pain ramped up. He writhed uselessly on the chair once more. The duct tape did not cede a tenth of an inch. He felt stupid and angry. He wasn't sure if he had been given anesthesia or other drugs, but the effects had started to fade away. The pain went up a level, a hammering sting that he knew, eventually, would have driven him crazy. He forced himself not to touch the spot again. He closed his eyes, hoping to push the pain away.

In the darkness of his mind, he met his dad. He imagined him spending his day in the garage, fixing old cars, heating his frozen TV meal, and killing a six-pack. He thought about his mother too—at least, the few memories of her that were still strong and colorful in his mind. He thought of his wife, and all the reasons why he'd decided to escape from her seemed somehow weaker now. He thought of the hitchhiker, and the old man. He thought of Greg, who was probably bombarding his phone with calls and messages.

Johnny Hawk had wanted to escape from everything and everyone—from the world; from himself. He had made himself purposely oblivious of everyone who had tried to reach him in the past weeks. Now, he yearned desperately for anyone who could take him out of the hole he had dug for himself.

His phone. He glanced down at his half-numb legs, looking

for the bulge in his front pocket. There was no trace of it, of course.

On the tray to his left, something gleamed, breaking his train of thought. The tray looked old and stained. He moved his left thumb, looking for the selector on the armrest. After a couple of attempts, the tray came alive, moving jerkily toward him. The closer it got, the clearer the horrific sight became. A sobbing moan choked in his throat, and at that point not only did he know he was going to die but that he was going to do so in a lot of pain. He shivered deep down inside his bones as the sun set, casting darkness preambles across the basement. The air felt heavier to breathe. *Everything looks worse than it is in the dark*, his dad's words came strong in his mind, *but the sun waits just behind the gloom.*

On the tray, a composition of objects had been organized with obsessive care, in a dreadfully symmetric scheme. A puzzle that didn't leave much room for interpretation. The reality of the message was second only to the power of it. He looked at the shadows getting longer on the walls, then glanced back at the tray.

Two five-dollar bills had been placed at the top corners of the tray. Just below the lower edge of each bill were the two incisors he was missing in his mouth. They had been placed on pieces of cotton, cut with tidy edges. Both the teeth had stained the cotton with small red dots of blood. The note went straight to the point. In a sharp-cornered handwriting, which he had seen before, the note read:

The Tooth Fairy takes
But she gives in return.
An honest trade with no guessing.
A trophy you must earn...

CHAPTER TWO:

TOOTHACHE

1

June 6, 2018

There were two moments from that cloudy and humid June evening that Johnny remembered very clearly. First, the pumping veins on Ellen's sweaty forehead, and second, the two red lights flashing at the top of the Chase Tower's antennae.

When his flight to Philadelphia got canceled earlier, he'd felt an unconscious sense of relief. This wasn't great for the business, but it was definitely good for his body and mind to have a little break. As he walked back from the Concourse A of Indianapolis International Airport, he thought about grabbing dinner and surprising Ellen. He could get a bottle of wine, maybe two. He couldn't remember the last time he'd had dinner with her.

The success of his software house company had increased

exponentially in the past months and so had his work hours. So, he used to find her asleep when he came home at night, and asleep she was the morning after when he had to leave for work. A quick kiss deposited on her forehead, brief texts during the day. That was all. Later, he would see things more clearly. That invisible way the fabric of relationships starts to loosen up, layer after layer, slipping out of control. Silent. Unconscious.

On that evening he got home around seven from the airport. Their apartment complex was a six-floor brick building with huge windows in all the rooms, a very good example of the post-industrial architecture that was invading the city, especially in the re-developed areas on the East side. The parking lot for residents was busy as always in the evening, so he parked on Walnuts Ave, jumped out of the car, and began to walk around the block toward the building entrance.

The heat outside was miserable. It was one of those ninety-five-degree Midwestern days, when it rains for ten seconds just to raise the humidity to the stars as the sun creeps back out. His back was sweaty, his shirt stuck to his skin. When he walked into the building's hall, the AC felt so good that he stopped there for a few seconds. His mind went to Arthur Jabber, better known as Art in his restricted and exclusive circle of friends. Even better known as the *motherfucker*. That nickname was Johnny's personal pick for him and for him only.

The motherfucker also happened to be his business partner. They co-founded and co-owned the Hawk-Jabber Tech Group. Many times, Johnny had wondered how his personal relationship with Art had deteriorated to this level, and the inevitable answer was always: money. The nickname had originated three years ago: the humble start-up they had started together was mature enough to step up to the next level. Capital increase, new clients signing big contracts, and old customers wanting more and more. More business meant more money but also the need to expand the company base and resources. Suddenly, everything became more difficult to manage, and harder to enjoy.

Johnny Hawk became the Chief Technical Officer of the company, overseeing all the technical areas, and Art—not yet the motherfucker; in fact, an actual brilliant and pleasant personality—became Chief Finance Officer. That marked the beginning of their relationship's decline. Johnny's vision for the company was to invest in new technologies to stay competitive against big tech corporations, but Art was keen to sacrifice the technical matters in order to maximize the profit. Johnny had promised himself that he would let Jabber know his nickname the day Johnny quit. So, three years had passed at that slow, steady, but relentless pace that only routine can create. After three years, he still worked with the motherfucker. There were still good days, but they had become rarer.

As he cooled down in the building's hall, an acute and stinging ache crossed the left side of his mouth. For a moment, he believed the motherfucker could hear his thoughts, sending back the toothache as a *Fuck you, Johnny! I hate you too.*

When he walked out of the elevator, he heard music coming

from his apartment. As he opened the door, he recognized Mick Jagger's rough voice invading the hallway. *Hot Rocks, side B, "Paint It Black."*

He was about to holler at Ellen, but the yell choked in his throat as a weird sound in the background caught his attention. A sort of whining, mixed with the snare of Charlie Watts's drum, hailing from the living room. Johnny stealthily placed the shopping bag on the floor and walked quietly down the hallway. He realized he was holding his breath. Something was not right, and his heart started to race so fast he could feel the pulse in his temples. The moaning became clearer as the music seemed to recede into the background, but his mind refused to understand. He stuck his head out to have a look.

On his wide, white ten-thousand-dollar daybed-style sofa, Ellen was naked, down on all fours, getting pounded by a tall muscular man wearing a black mask.

His first thought was that Ellen was being assaulted, but then he looked at Ellen in the mirror and saw the intense pleasure painted on her face. She wanted it. She was enjoying it. As the foundations of his entire world trembled, his mind went to all the most irrelevant places. For example, he would have never imagined that Ellen liked that kind of stuff, the submission, the fetish part of it. It made him doubt deeply how much he knew about her.

An intense sense of nausea clenched his stomach. He felt dizzy. He hid behind the wall, resting his back on it, and had to brace himself against the door jamb. The music was loud and clear, but the sounds seemed to be padded in his head. He was desperately trying to isolate himself from the lovers' pleasure. He peeked again, unsure of what he wanted to do, or what he could do, but willing he wanted to remain unseen.

Ellen's eyes were closed. She wore a black leather collar with a chain attached. The man behind her was controlling the tension in the chain. The more he pulled on it, the more she seemed to enjoy it. The veins stood out on her forehead, drawing a V-shape. He had noticed them popping like that before, after she went for a run, but never when they made love. Her breasts swung with each thrust. The sound of their skin smacking together. And Johnny stood there, at the living room entrance.

Invisible.

He listened to the sound of her pleasure growing. At some point, the man with the mask pulled the chain hard, grabbing her hair with his right hand. When Johnny's wife shouted out, proclaiming her climax, he decided it was time to go. He wasn't sure how much time he had been standing there, but it didn't matter.

The music ended, and the room was filled with the scraping sound of the turntable needle and the moaning of the lovers. Johnny left his apartment for the last time, making sure not to make a sound when he closed the door at his back.

A moment later, he slammed his car door behind him and sat, panting heavily. He was hyperventilating, so he decided to focus on one spot in space and work on his breathing. That was when he saw the blinking lights. Through the windshield, far off in the distance, as the sunlight faded, leaving pink and orange lacerations in the sky, two slim antennas stuck upward from the Chase Tower's roof. Those relentless blinking red eyes stared at him, hypnotizing him. The regular flickering slowed everything around him down. These eyes watched the city, knowing everything and everyone, yet powerless. And so was he, unable to move a muscle, with his heart running fast in his chest, a voiceless spectator in a red-light theatre that was playing the movie about the failure of his life. There wasn't sadness or anger. Just emptiness and disbelief. And those blinking lights.

He had once read that every person in the world, at some stage of their existence, is likely to have a breakdown, a fatal error in the system, a hard reset, a life-changing event that shuffles all the cards in the deck. And he knew right away this was his own personal fatal error. Amid the panic and all the random thoughts, he couldn't have seen things more clearly. It was almost like all the discomfort brought a much-deserved clarity along.

Later, as time passed, he might have forgotten the veins on Ellen's forehead, pumping blood at the same rate of her pleasure. But there was no way he could've removed those two lights from his mind. Red eyes blinking in an eternal loop. They had always been there.

But Johnny Hawk saw them on that night, for the first time.

2

June 20th, 2018

Two weeks later the phone buzzed on the nightstand at 10:00 a.m. Johnny slammed it with his right hand to stop it and took his time to welcome another shitty day. Eventually, he got up and walked barefoot over the dusty carpet to the bathroom to urinate. He had gotten used to the smoky smell of room 214, which must have been a smoking room back in the day, at least until someone decided that blowing a pack of cigarettes in a five-hundred-square-feet-shithole was not tolerated anymore.

He had also gotten used to the slimy dirt between the green-vomit-colored tiles, which covered the walls and floor in the bathroom and which he noticed every time he was there. But for the Lord's sake, he couldn't get used to the beep sound the clock produced every time the hour changed. 3:00 a.m., *beep*, 4:00 a.m., *beep*. That damn thing was driving him nuts. He was pretty sure he heard it even while dreaming. He didn't mind it anymore, though. It had become part of the self-punishment.

Actually, he had started appreciating all the little discomforts that only a mid-western cheap hotel could offer. He needed the discomforts now, to purify himself after all the comfortable shit that had made him blind. He could have afforded a five-star hotel. He could've bought a house with a swimming pool in the best neighborhood in the city if he had wanted, but he knew that wasn't what he needed. He needed to go back all the way to real life. At least, that was what he kept telling himself.

He walked to the sink, which was in the same room where his bed was, threw some cold water on his face, and brushed his teeth. When he rinsed, an acute pain thumped in the left side of his mouth. An electric shock that took his breath away for a fraction of a second. Then the pain was gone, leaving him with a funny face in front of the mirror. *You'd better take care of that damn tooth, Johnny boy*, he told himself, realizing he hadn't visited a dentist in at least five years. *I'll take care of it later*, he thought. More important things were on the horizon now.

He looked at his phone, which he had forgotten to charge the night before. It showed a residual 17 percent of battery, six missed calls, and fourteen unread text messages. He knew who was trying to reach him, but he checked anyway. Four out of six were from Ellen. An equal number of messages were left in the voicemail. Without even listening, he deleted all the messages from her. He hadn't communicated with her in any form since he'd found her fucking the black-masked man and, for right now, he was happy to keep it that way. *Let her cook in her own broth*, he told himself. Since he'd gone MIA, no one had called the police, and that was good because he didn't have to explain shit. Ellen must have known she had been busted because he'd left the grocery bags at the door before leaving the apartment.

In the first few days after the fact, he had called his dad once. He knew Ellen would call him and he didn't want to worry him unnecessarily. He just didn't want to hear the bitch's voice anymore. He was aware he would have to talk to her eventually, even if it was to kick her out of the house or divorce her, but there was no rush, desire, or need at the present time. He could almost picture her, looking out the window in their luxury condo downtown, holding a cup of green tea, ashamed, aware that her husband knew. He knew everything now.

The sixth missed call was from Gregory Bollard. He must have forgotten the three-hour time difference between Los Angeles and Indianapolis since he'd tried to call at 1:34 a.m. He had left a message on the voicemail. Greg was the only other person he had talked to about it. Johnny had told him the whole story.

Johnny reached the short fridge, placed below a 20" TV screen made by some unpronounceable Korean brand. He opened the fridge and jumped back when a spider darted out. He grabbed a can of Budweiser from the six-pack he had gotten the night before when he'd been way too tipsy to notice that "America" had replaced the usual Budweiser logo. He opened the can and took the first sip of the day. He sat on the bed and lit up a Marlboro Silver. He judged, based on the smell of that place, the no smoking sign was more of a decorative element than a motel policy. What was important anymore?

With his elbows propped on his naked legs, his chin resting in his hands, he played Gregory's message on speaker.

"Hey, it's Greg. Haven't heard back from you in a week. Is everything alright? Uhm...I mean I know it's not alright. Just wondering if you're still planning to come here. I will be out of

town next week. I have to visit a client in Malaysia on Tuesday. I'll be back in L.A. on Friday morning. Not sure if my phone will work while I'm gone, just in case you try to reach me." He paused.

"Hey, listen. I know this must be very tough. Just keep your shit together. I still can't believe you want to call out from H&J. Did you talk with Art already? I mean, man—are you sure of what you're doing? Isn't it a little too impulsive? There is a potential shitload of money on the table. You know my door's always open for you. Just in case you decide to come here while I'm away, I'll leave the keys in the usual spot. Hawk... I just want you to know we'll figure it out. Just don't mess around. And please pick up your goddamned phone. Let me know you're still fucking breathing. Call me back."

Johnny found himself smiling when the message ended. The worried tone of his friend's voice consoled him a bit. Made him feel a little less shitty. *Someone still cares*, he thought. If there was still a breathing human being on Earth who really cared, always had, that was Greg. That thought made him realize that the feeling was not only mutual but exclusive too. Greg was really the only person Johnny cared about. He could now see, more clearly, his slice of blame for the deterioration of all his personal relationships. Ellen's betrayal had opened his eyes wide on the kind of person he was. His arrogance emerged as if he was looking at a selfish prick from the outside. He could see the mask that he had built for himself. It didn't justify Ellen's behavior, but he could understand why she did it. Brief texts during the day, rude answers during their fights, and a whole lot of indifference were the only things he had given her in recent times.

Johnny texted Greg back that he was fine and would call him soon. He was still planning to visit him soon, no specific dates. Reluctantly, he added a smiley face at the end. Wasn't that the new fucked-up way society wanted you to let people know you were fine?

He finished his beer and crumpled the can, tossing it into the trash full of other cans. When he'd checked in ten days before, the door hanger had been, of course, two-sided. One side was red with white letters saying *Do not disturb! If you know what I mean.* On the bottom was a re-interpretation of the road work sign, showing two people copulating. The back side was white and said *Please make up my room! Sorry for the mess.* He had left the hanger always on the red side, though not because he was having fun with anyone. Getting laid was his last thought these days. Sometimes the picture of his wife's face with her eyes closed and her mouth hanging open gave him a boner, and sometimes it made him want to throw up.

Sometimes both.

3

He put on a light green tee-shirt and a pair of jeans and gathered all his stuff in a blue Nike gym bag. When he left the room, a burst of heat and humidity slapped him right in his face. The

AC units hummed loudly in the still air. His head throbbed, and the left part of his mouth was sore. He threw the bag in the trunk of his car and walked to the reception area. A warbling sound welcomed him when he opened the door. The front desk was empty. A very large man in a Hawaiian shirt popped out from a door behind the desk, chewing as he rushed to the counter.

"Morning, how can I help you?" the man asked. Hanging from the light-blue shirt with white flowers was a fake silver tag, which read: *Donald, Front desk assistant.*

"Checking out," Johnny replied, looking at Donald's red mustache, dirty with gravy.

"Sure," Donald said and started typing. His labored breath was the only sound in the room. A couple of minutes later the receptionist came back with a printed receipt.

"Is there anything else I can help you with?" Donald panted like he'd just run a 5k, eager to go back to his breakfast.

"No. Thank you."

4

Johnny's schedule was full for the day, and the appointment he had at noon was the most important one. Getting out of the motel after days of loneliness felt weird. Walking downtown in the morning was something he never had the chance to do. How many times in the past five years had he taken a day off?

How many nights had he stayed late at work trying to keep the business going, especially in the hard times? It felt good to realize that now, he had all the time in the world, and he intended to use it properly.

He parked his car three blocks away from the place where he was supposed to have his meeting. Despite the thick, hot air, he wanted to walk. His new style was different from his usual suit and tie. He looked at his watch: 11.48 a.m. Downtown Indy was busy with people rushing to their lunches. A block past his car, he saw the famous St. Elmo Steakhouse, a real institution in Indy. Standing since 1902 and, as a matter of fact, one of his favorite restaurants. Too bad he was always there for business and never for leisure. *When was the last time I took Ellen to have a shrimp cocktail and a filet*? He wondered as he glanced at the people inside, sitting at their fancy tables, eating their sixty-dollar filet mignons, medium rare. He could see himself from outside, right there, trying to convince a client to buy his new cyber-security package or explaining how he had prototyped a new machine learning algorithm. He could see the person he was before sitting right there, and he could imagine that man glimpsing the new him glaring in those thoroughly cleaned windows. He felt sick and grateful at the same time.

He walked two more blocks south and stopped in front of a small orange building. A little black board leaning on the street read: *Mind your biscuit and your life will be gravy.* An uncontrollable grin appeared on his face as he thought about the person he was about to meet, sitting in a low-end diner, all dressed up. As he smiled, he felt his left cheek expanding from the inside. He passed his tongue against it, tasting a bloody tang in his saliva. That damn tooth again. He needed to take care of it ASAP.

He stepped inside. The place was long and narrow, with a row of tables and booths on the right side. On the left side of the room was the cash register and the kitchen. The place was dead despite the rush hour. There was no AC, only three fans on the roof swirling at medium speed. He noticed two kids who had probably ditched school, eating French fries at the very end of the diner. At another table, four large men, all wearing veteran caps, played cards with their mugs stuck in their hands. The other tables were empty. There was no music on, the only sound was the sizzling hiss of raw meat and vegetables on the grill.

Johnny sat and placed his keys and phone on the table. The waitress, a young Latina woman in her late twenties, hair fixed in a ponytail, came to the table to take his order. She announced that the special of the day was a chicken quesadilla for eight bucks. He ordered a coffee and told her he was waiting for another person shortly. He had been there for less than five minutes and already smelled like he had bathed in frying oil.

This is going to piss him off all right, he thought proudly as another involuntary grin popped up on his face. The waitress came back with his coffee just as a large, tall man in an elegant suit sat across from him in the booth.

The man watched Johnny with hateful eyes. He was panting,

and his face was red and sweaty. He laid his overnight case on the booth, still staring. His lower jaw was tight, making him look like a mad bulldog.

After a time, the man pointed his finger at Johnny, shaking with rage.

"Where the fuck have you been? I called you something like one hundred times. And what is this shithole? Couldn't we meet at the usual place?"

"Nice seeing you too, Art," Johnny said calmly, sipping his coffee–which, by the way, was incredibly good. Talking with the motherfucker now, he felt an unusual sense of ease for the first time in a long time. Arthur took a deep breath, trying to compose himself.

"Are you going to tell me why you didn't come back from Philadelphia with the Cunningham contract signed? Are you going to tell me why you didn't even go there?"

"Calm down, Art—"

"Don't fucking tell me to calm down, Johnny." Art slammed his hand on the table. "You were missing for ten fucking days. I need an explanation, and it had better be a good one."

Johnny sighed. He could feel his heartbeat accelerating and his repulsion dangerously increasing. He forced himself to keep calm.

"Listen, Art; I've got some issues at home. Some pretty bad ones."

The waiters came back to take Arthur's order.

"Just a glass of water, please," Jabber said, attempting a weak and circumstantial smile. He turned his focus back to Johnny. "What happened? I left you I don't know how many messages."

Johnny took another sip of his coffee. The hot liquid caused a stabbing pain in the left side of his mouth. He instinctively pressed a hand on his left jowl. His beard was a couple of weeks long, and for a second, it felt like petting a porcupine.

"I'm done, Arthur. I'm leaving."

Jabber laughed soundly.

"Is that right?" he replied, amused. "And how exactly are you planning to do that?"

When the two of them founded the company, the split was fifty-fifty. One year later Jabber asked if he could buy another slice from Johnny's half. Johnny had eventually agreed, selling him an additional ten percent, which made Jabber the majority shareholder in terms of pure percentages. Johnny knew that Jabber had anticipated this moment for a long time. He always had dreamed about being the sole owner. The point was not if he could cash out Johnny's part. The point was how much money he was available to pay for it.

"I know we've had our difficulties, but it's nothing personal. I need to leave town, and I will need to cash out my slice."

Jabber looked at him, sighing. For a moment Johnny could even see a crumb of empathy in his eyes.

"Are you in trouble with the law? The last thing I need is IRS people or FBI walking in the office."

"I'm clean, and there's nothing illegal in cashing out my part."

Jabber took a sip of his coffee and sighed again, looking out of the window on his right.

"Are you out of your goddamn mind, Hawk? I mean, you know you're going to lose a shitload of money, right? Not that it matters to me, but I've never heard of such a dumb move in my whole career. I'm telling you this against my own interest. Do you realize how much you are leaving on the table? Not to mention the penalty for breach of contract. I mean, I'm not your damn financial advisor. You can take some time off and still be—"

"I need to cash out! I've done the math," he said, hardly realizing he had hit the table with his fist. The diffuse background noise of the kitchenware stopped, leaving an odd quiet in the diner. Johnny didn't have to turn to know he was being observed. Then, everything went back to normal.

Jabber kept looking at him. A quality Johnny had always admired of him.

"Alright, alright," he said after a while. "I hope you know what you're doing, Johnny." He rarely called him Johnny. Only when they were at dinner with important clients, to pretend a close relationship. And again that feeling of self-realization hit him. For the second time on that day he could watch himself from the outside. *How have I become such an arrogant prick? There was a time when we called one another by name. A time when things were simpler and more exciting.* Images of the past flashed through Johnny's mind. He saw himself cutting the wires of his relationship with Arthur. He felt a sense of guilt and nostalgia mixed together. Again, he felt his part of responsibility for things had gone. But that was the past and it was too late anyway. Not a good moment to go soft. Not right now.

"Ballpark?" Arthur asked, sipping his water.

Johnny's heart increased its pace. It was time to spit out the number—and he was sure Jabber would use all his negotiation skills. He was undoubtedly good at that, and Johnny was not. That's why Johnny wrote the code and Jabber closed the deals. The left part of his mouth ached. *Okay, Johnny boy. Hold your balls in your hands and just spit it out.*

"Two point seven," Johnny finally said.

Jabber's laughter was loud and sudden. Johnny had seen that coming, no matter what number he might've asked for. He had pictured this scene over and over in his mind and, so far, Jabber had played his part. Two point seven was an optimistic number, but he thought it was a good starting point.

"You can't possibly be serious, Hawk."

"I'm a hundred percent serious, Art. That's how much you need to buy my slice. I've done the math. The company is growing fast, and we had three point two million in revenues only last year. I'm aware this is the worst moment to cash out, but I need to leave, and I need the money."

Jabber's bald, round head was red. He loosened the collar of his shirt. That was a good sign.

"You can't be serious," he repeated. "It's not my problem if you'll need to pay fees and a penalty. Do you understand that? What is the fairest you can do? Try again."

"Two point seven million, Arthur. That's the fairest I can do."

"I think a fair number is closer to one point five. After all, you'll still get to keep more than a meal ticket."

"I don't think you're listening to me, Arthur. Let me explain this a little more plainly. Our company has a potential ten-million-dollar value today, and this number is going to increase. My slice is forty percent of it. I think I'm being very fucking generous here."

"I think you should also consider what happened last year in Indonesia. You remember, Art, don't you? I'm not sure you had the chance to talk with your wife about that." Johnny didn't want to really play this card, but the situation, as expected, required a little bit more than pure negotiation skills.

"Are you threatening me, Hawk?"

Johnny didn't respond.

"Go home, Johnny. You don't seem to be yourself today."

"My offer is not going to change. I'm expecting your lawyer to call me before the end of the day," Johnny said.

"What the hell is the matter with you, Johnny? What about Ellen? Does she even know about it?"

Johnny stood up, threw a twenty-dollar bill on the table, and looked Jabber straight in the face. "You tell your lawyer to call me." Then he walked away.

"*Where* the hell are you going, Hawk? You can't threaten me like that," Jabber yelled at him.

He didn't turn back. His heart pounded in his chest, the pain throbbed in his mouth, and spread to his head as the adrenaline flowed in his legs. When he reached his car, he realized he was running.

He sat in his car. He let the heat hit him right in the face, feeling the sweat at the base of his neck, waiting for his heart to slow down. Ten minutes later, he placed his phone in the magnetic holder on the dash and said: "Hey, Siri!"

The automatic voice asked how she could help him.

"Take me to the closest CVS."

5

Two hours later, he cruised along a gravel driveway. Tall oaks stood on either side of the driveway, projecting a nice shade, which Johnny was able to feel even inside the car as scattered memories, sounds, and smells from his childhood arose. He remembered walking with his mom to place red balloons on the mailbox. Those were for his birthday, which was at the beginning of summer, right around this time. The driveway was long and curvy. At the end of it was a two-floor house, which hadn't changed at all, except for some siding planks on the attic, which had started to show the paint's age.

A tall, broad man in a navy tee was reading a book, on a red wooden swing under the shade of the tall trees. He put the book down and stood up, with the aid of a stick, as Johnny got out of the car. The man, who clearly hadn't been expecting any visitors, stood with his right hand like a visor on his forehead, trying to scrutinize the cutout of the visitor in the bright June sun.

"How's it going, Dad?" Johnny yelled at him.

The man's features relaxed. The wrinkles on his forehead, which were even deeper than Johnny remembered, arched with surprise.

"Johnny?"

"In the flesh!" His voice trembled a bit when his dad hugged him.

"I wasn't expecting you. Are you alright?"

"I'm good. Not too bad. I was in the area and thought I'd say hi."

Peter Hawk nodded, but his eyes told Johnny that he couldn't fool his old man, not that easily. It must have been that parent radar thing. That one sixth sense.

"Let's go inside. I'll get you something to drink."

The cool air felt good as they walked in. The house was in decent shape. Some furniture had been moved around; Johnny couldn't tell what exactly, but the living room area looked off. The kitchen bar had only two stools, not four like when they all used to have breakfast before school. A tiny layer of dust stuck to his fingertips when he passed his hand over the white marble countertop.

"How's Jennifer?"

"She's alright. She only comes to clean on Wednesday now. This house doesn't need so much cleaning anymore, and I could use the money for other things. She offered to come over on Friday too, for free, but I wouldn't let her. I guess she loves this house. More than I do anyway. You know I practically live in the garage."

"Some things never change." Johnny smiled at his dad. In the kitchen light, he realized how much the old man had aged since the last time he had seen him.

"What happened to your face? Did your barber die?" Peter Hawk snickered. Johnny smiled, touching his beard.

"You know, beards are trendy nowadays, Dad. You should think about growing one."

"Do you want a beer? I've got some cold ones."

Johnny sat on the stool on the far left, the same one he used to sit on for breakfast before school. That kitchen had been much more crowded and louder. He could still see his mom making French toast on the stove, and his sister arguing with him about using her things without asking. That room, once full of people and love, was now empty and silent. Nonetheless, he could still feel the warmth of that place, the atmosphere that was there every year for Christmas Eve or Thanksgiving.

He twisted his beer open and took a sip. It felt so good to scrape the dry from his throat, but his goddamn tooth started throbbing like hell again as soon as the cold reached it. The pain flared in his nerves, and he closed his eyes for a second, waiting for it to pass.

"So, what brings you here today, son?"

"What do you mean? I told you, I was driving by and—"

"You know, Johnny, I think I'm grown enough for you to cut the shit and get straight to the point. It's been three months since I have heard from you or Ellen. Your sister lives on the other side of the country, but she still calls and talks to me more than you do. So, pardon my skepticism, but: is something going on that I should know, son?"

Johnny told him what happened with Ellen, omitting the details. It was already shameful enough. His dad looked at him without saying anything. By the time Johnny finished explaining the situation, they had killed another beer each.

"I'm going to leave for a while, Dad. Probably tomorrow. I need a place to crash for the night, if that's okay with you."

"This is your home, Johnny. And always will be. You don't even have to ask."

"Thanks."

"Where are you headed?"

"I thought I'd go see Greg in L.A. He always tells me there are opportunities down there. And the weather is nice. Actually, the main reason I'm leaving is so that I don't have to worry about scraping the ice from the goddamn windshield every morning."

His dad chuckled, and then his features went serious again.

"Are you sure of what you're doing, Johnny? I mean, is there any chance you can sort things out with Ellen? Marriage is complicated. I guess you know that. I had some bad times with your mom, too."

"What times?" Johnny asked with genuine curiosity.

Peter sighed and then grinned, as if the memory he was trying to recall was bittersweet. He cleared his throat.

"There's no easy way to say this. When you were two years old, your mom had a bad period. I was working for TrueSport that year, and it was kind of a big deal with the new car for the Indy 500 race on that particular year. I was working on Bobby Rahal's car. We worked like hell that May, something like eighteen hours a day. There was no night and day. There were no weekends. Most of the time, when I got back home, your mom was already asleep. Sometimes I even slept at the racetrack with the other guys. Of course, your mom was not happy with that. But I kept telling her that year we really had a chance to win. That didn't seem to help. Some women don't like to be lonely. Hell, nobody likes to be lonely."

"What happened?"

"Well, you know that we won the Indy 500 that year. But you probably don't know that your mom didn't show up at the celebration. I don't think she even watched the race." He took a long sip. "A week later, I saw her driving and followed her to a nearby motel. That's how I found out."

"You gotta be kidding me. Mom? There's no way."

"It was a tough time, son, the toughest of my life. But eventually, we sorted things out. You know, back in those days there was no couples' therapy crap or any of that stuff. I've always liked to fix things, but that was, without a doubt, the hardest thing I've ever had to fix. But we did it. And we did it because of you, Johnny. Then your sisters came, and we learned new ways to love each other, to fight with each other, to stand up for each other. And that was the best choice I've ever made in life. We were together for forty years. Ironically, I think her affair completely changed the idea I used to have about love. People are complicated, but see, things can be fixed sometimes. Don't need to throw it away."

Johnny's shock was numbed by the beer, which was starting to kick in. Still, he couldn't believe what he had just heard.

"I'm sorry, Dad. To hear that, I mean. It must be a family curse."

His father didn't respond to that. "Why don't you go get your stuff from the car? Are you hungry? We could order some pizza."

"I was afraid you'd never ask."

6

They ate their pizza and drank more beer sitting in the wooden outdoor chairs on the rear patio. The sun was setting and the sky seemed about to catch on fire, shading orange and red tones all over the scattered clouds. They sat there conjuring the old days—the funny moments and the sad ones. It was a nice time. The best Johnny could remember having with his dad. The memories that he had of his dad, always reserved and introvert during Johnny's childhood, clashed with the image of what their relationship had become. He had the sensation of talking with a wise friend.

Johnny stood up and leaned on the patio fence. He looked around, almost able to see himself, Maggie, Susan, and Klara running in the grass. Hiding behind the massive weeping willow tree and building their fort with an old tent.

He lit a cigarette and exhaled deeply.

"I guess you know how hard it is to get rid of those coffin nails, don't you?" Peter uttered, passing one hand through his thin white hair. "It took me thirty years to quit, and I could still eat one."

Johnny nodded, took another hit, and kept spacing out in the bloody-orange sky.

"So, are you really doing this?" Peter asked with a thin but perceptible note of concern.

Johnny realized that he wasn't so sure anymore. The thought that he was overreacting slipped into his mind. It suddenly looked so easy to just move out from his house (which he practically already had) and keep his business rather than trying to restart from a clean slate. At the same time, he still felt that new sense of freedom that he hadn't known in years, and he didn't want to give up on it that easily. Deep inside him he thought there was something to learn out of all this. He liked to picture all those paths and opportunities out there and the thrill of not knowing where he would be in five years.

"I need a change of scenery."

"When, son?"

He had no idea on how to respond to that. He didn't have a plan, or even a plane ticket.

A buzzing sound coming from his left pocket disrupted his thoughts. Clifton Sticks, the company lawyer. Johnny waited a couple of more purrs, took a deep breath, and answered.

"Hello?"

"*Johnny; Clifton here.*" The voice at the other end of the phone was as deep as he expected.

"How're you doing, bud? What's up?"

"*Listen, I don't know if there's a mistake or a misunderstanding here, but I've just gotten off the phone with Arthur. He emailed me a cash-out proposal. Is that right?*"

"I guess it depends on what the proposal says, Cliff." He could hear his heartbeat in his ears. He didn't expect Arthur to move so quickly. It could be a very good thing or a very bad one. Fifty-fifty.

"*Two point three.*"

Johnny stood with his phone in his right hand and the cigarette in the other. The ash had accumulated, forming a long hook. He stood there silently and felt the sweat leaking at the base of his neck. He had asked for two point seven million, and Jabber had come out four hundred thousand shy, but he'd expected that. Honestly, he would have accepted anything above two million.

He looked at his pop.

"Then I guess it's right. You can go ahead and formalize it.

Can you use my electronic signature?" he said, trying to mask his childish excitement.

"*Johnny, are you ACTUALLY cashing out your slice? You're going to pay nearly three hundred grand in penalties and—*"

"Cliff, I'm sorry I didn't speak with you before, but I'm done."

There was a long pause on the other end. Johnny liked Cliff. He was a damn good attorney and a really nice guy— but Johnny's mind was already tasting his personal victory over Arthur Jabber, and the incredible feeling of not having anything to do with that man anymore. That was the real price. That was it.

"*It's fine by me; do you want me to transfer everything on your account?*"

"Yes, please."

"*Alright. Just so you know, it's going to take a couple of weeks before you see that money. I'll need to file all the IRS stuff first.*"

"You do what you gotta do, Cliff. And thanks, man, for everything. Take care of yourself."

He hung up and looked at his dad, who was giving him the classic look of someone who wants to know what the hell is going on.

"I've just pissed on half a million dollars, Dad, and you know what?"

"What?"

"It feels incredible."

7

"Come with me, Johnny. I want to show you something."

Johnny followed his dad through the rear patio into the kitchen, then to the door leading to the garage. Johnny knew what this was about. Of course he knew; there weren't many things Peter Hawk was really passionate about. He looked back at his son with excited eyes. No question his eyes were older, more tired, more sad, more aware, but they still sparkled with the same light.

Peter turned on the lights. The room had been recently painted. It looked better than the house itself. The stainless-steel-top counters lining the room shone like diamonds. On the left corner against the wall was a huge red metallic box. Johnny remembered his dad yelling at him not to mess with the red toolbox when he was a kid. That was a long time ago, a time that had seemed *happy*. Things had changed. The toolbox was still the same. Immutable.

Something like fifty wrenches hung on the wall behind the toolbox, arranged from the smallest size to the biggest with maniacal harmony. That was Peter Hawk. Everything came down to racing cars. On the opposite wall, an uncountable number of frames showed him with A.J. Foyt, Dale Earnhardt, Ayrton Senna, you name it. In a dark, shiny brown frame, there was a picture of Peter on the 24 Hours of Le Mans finish line. That garage was his legacy. It kept the memories of a life.

In the middle of the room stood a hulking mass in the shape of a car. A silky purple cloth covered it, reflecting the neon lights like a dress on a curvy lady. Johnny opened his eyes wide with disbelief.

"Is that what I think it is?" He brought both his hands to his mouth.

"It is, Johnny. It is," Peter said with his arms crossed, looking at his creature with the proudest grin.

Not more than two years ago, Johnny's dad was struggling to find a few rare parts. Johnny could remember him stuck at the phone during Christmas holidays, calling spare parts sellers in England, looking online for every possible deal.

"When did you finish it?"

"Last week. It's funny, I was going to call you one of these days to come see it. Good thing you stopped by before leaving."

His dad grabbed one end of the cloth and unveiled the car. Peter had shown Johnny so many pictures and videos, told him so many stories and details, that he knew practically every secret of this car already. But when he saw it right there in front of him, he understood. Suddenly everything Peter had told him about this car made sense.

The English-racing-green 1963 Jaguar - XKE was stunning, perfection in shape. Johnny and his dad had always agreed that it was the most beautiful car ever produced. It gleamed under the garage's lights with striking beauty. Each line, each curve, and chromium plate merged in a divine balance of agility and lightness. The interior was red leather with clamshell seats. An aluminum central bridge hosted the manual gear shift lever. Four gears plus reverse. The steering wheel had a mahogany rim.

"Can I sit in it?" Johnny asked timidly.

"Are you really asking?" Peter giggled. "*Madeline* has nothing against being sat in." His laughter echoed in the room.

Johnny sat in the driver's seat while Peter took the passenger side. Johnny felt the smooth mahogany with the fingertips. Then he tried a solid hold.

"It's perfect, Dad. Just like you wanted it. How did you do it in such a short time? I mean, it's beautiful."

"It's not that much work, Johnny. Most of the parts just needed some elbow grease. The previous owner was an old lady who bought the car in 1963, and I have to say, she kept it immaculate. I just cleaned it, did some metal polish, and it slowly came all together. Of course, I had to replace some parts for safety. But the engine is still the original one. It's like new. Doesn't even have twenty thousand miles. If you went back in time to 1963, you would've gotten exactly what you're sitting on."

"What are you going to do with it? I bet you could sell it for a lot—"

"There's no way I'm going to sell this." Peter raised his voice, sounding almost angry. "See, things aren't just made to be sold, Johnny. I want this thing to see the road."

"Sure, that makes sense."

"You didn't answer my question earlier."

"What question?"

"Are you leaving tomorrow then?"

"Yep, I think so. Actually, would you mind giving me a ride to the airport?"

Peter didn't respond to that. He sighed in the way fathers do when they need to let their sons go. Again.

"If it's a problem, I can just Uber; it's not a big—"

"Why don't you drive? I mean, that's what I would do if I wanted some time with me, myself, and I. The road. There's no such medicine for the soul."

He thought about it, seriously considering the option. There was the cold and rational side that couldn't see a reason to waste so much time on the road.

But he *had* time now. Time was all he had craved for so long. The other voice in his head was the one that had rested silently, numbly, for years. The one he hadn't followed. Ever.

"I don't know. I mean, it sounds a little crazy."

"Do you want to hear another crazy one?"

"Go for it."

"You should take *Madeline* with you."

8

June 21, 2018

The night went fast. A nine-hour sleep with no dreams. A rare moment of pure rest. Johnny woke up to a metallic clattering of silverware and pans coming from the kitchen. He looked at his phone and walked to the bathroom.

It had been a while since he slept this well. He whistled over the melody of his urine diving into the toilet. His mouth had a horrible taste, something between an ashtray, blood, and a rotting mouse. Hell, it was really bad. He went to the sink to rinse it out, forgetting how cold water didn't get along with his teeth lately. As soon as the water touched the gums on the left side, a stinging pain raged for a second, which seemed never-ending. Then it settled. When he spat, a branched gush of blood mixed with the saliva that landed in the sink. He rinsed again, and this time it was more saliva than blood. He kept rinsing until there was no blood. He could feel a little bump on his gum when he passed the tongue on it. It tasted salty. He imposed himself not to tongue it more than necessary, knowing this was more or less like telling yourself not to think about an elephant.

He took a shower and got dressed, packed his things, and went downstairs.

Peter was in the kitchen, clumsily trying to manage three different pans on the stove.

"That smells good!" Johnny said, sitting on one of the black stools.

"Good morning!" Peter responded animatedly. "Did you sleep alright?"

"Like a baby. I feel reborn!"

"There's some fresh coffee over there," he said, pointing to the counter with a spatula. "You hungry?"

"Always!"

Peter turned off the stove and brought two plates back to the bar. French toast, bacon, and scrambled eggs. He looked really excited.

"Look. I know it sounds crazy, but the more I think about it, the more I realize you should take it."

Johnny looked at him unperturbed, still plastered from the long sleep, chewing mechanically with the right side of his mouth. He bet the old man had passed all night thinking about it, despite that Johnny had gently declined the offer to take the Jaguar across the country. He had already removed it from the options. To be honest, he thought the beer was speaking on behalf of his dad.

"What are you talking about?" Johnny said, pretending not to know the topic of the conversation.

"The car, Johnny. Madeline. I insist that you drive it to L.A. for your trip."

"I don't think I can, Dad. I mean, I'd be worried about it all the time."

"My baby needs to see the road, Johnny. She was built to be seen and to see. I thought about going on a trip myself, but it's not easy for me."

Johnny kept chewing, head down.

"This French toast is amaz—"

"I'm serious. I'm giving you the chance to take her on a trip to L.A."

"The trip is long. I'll be away for months. What if something breaks?"

"Alright; now you're offending me. The car is going to be just fine."

Johnny took a long breath, shaking his head. The cold part was rooting for his comfortable and reliable BMW, not for daddy's jewel. What if something did break? Where the hell was he going to find spare parts for a 1963 Jaguar? The hot part was quivering about the idea of driving a convertible Jaguar through the desert. The "new" Johnny was really attracted by the idea.

"Are you sure? You worked on it for years."

"All that time would be so worthless if this beauty didn't hit the road."

Johnny felt nervous and honored at the same time. But most of all, he felt free. He raised his coffee mug in a toast. For the first time after two weeks, Johnny felt that today was a better day than yesterday had been.

"Well. I guess I'll take your baby on a trip."

CHAPTER THREE:

HAPPY BIRTHDAY

1

June 13th, 1993

Twenty-five years before Johnny Hawk got ready to cross the United States in a 1963 Jaguar XKE, Wendy Jag woke up in her bed, covered in sweat. She didn't know if she had screamed, but she could still remember the nightmare she'd just had. It was always the same, the swing and the stars. Once, she had thought that since the nightmare was always the same, it might get less scary with time. As if getting used to bad things helped make them less bad. But now, at the age of seven, she had realized that the mind doesn't work like that.

She sat on the edge of her bed panting and reached for the glass of water on her nightstand. The clock on the wall was loud as usual with its rhythmic clacking. 6:45 a.m. She hoped she didn't wake Daddy up. Waking Daddy up on an early Monday morning was a very bad idea, since it was his day off. He was a dentist—the best in Copper City, she used to tell the kids at school. They usually quipped that he was the worst, too, being the only one in town.

That terrible dream still perched in the back of her mind. She had another sip of water and landed again on her pillow. *It wasn't real, it wasn't real,* she whispered to Ben. Ben couldn't respond to that, as he was a stuffed brown bear. Ben stared at her with lifeless black eyes.

"Do you think my daddy's dead," she whispered in Ben's soft ear.

Ben didn't answer.

"Should I go check if he's alive?"

Ben didn't answer that either, but she could almost hear him telling her to be careful and not to wake him up. Because he could get mad. And she knew what that meant.

"I'm just going to see if he's breathing. You wait for me here."

Ben fell back on the bed, his black eyes glistening. Wendy opened the door and took a quick look down the dark hallway. All the doors were kept closed—that was one of Daddy's rules. The old planks creaked as she started walking, despite her light weight. She put a finger on her mouth, reminding herself to be quiet. She passed the bathroom door on her right.

She went on until the next door: Daddy's bedroom. It had been left ajar, which happened sometimes when Daddy was too tired or had drunk too much. She peeked through the gap, but the wall impeded a clear visual of the bed. She grabbed the edge of the door and pushed it gently.

As the door moved, the hinges squeaked, loudly and unexpectedly. She brought both her hands to her mouth, terrified. Her heart leaped in her chest when she saw the shape under the blanket moving.

The room was dark and smelled like cigarettes. Daddy rolled over but didn't wake up. He found a new position and kept on snoring hard.

She relaxed and felt glad. Her daddy was still breathing and there was no white froth on the sides of his mouth. Moreover, she hadn't woken him up. She didn't close the door, not wanting to risk another squeak, so she crept back to her bedroom and got dressed.

When she was done, she tucked Ben under her arm and went to the kitchen. The sweet, intense smell of garbage welcomed her. She held her nose and took the black bag resting on the ground outside to the trash can. She wasn't strong or tall enough to raise it and throw it in, so she rested it next to the can.

She went back in. The smell was less intense but still there. She opened the fridge and poured some milk in a cup, and then she grabbed a handful of cereal from a pink box. On the box, there was a cow that poured milk with one hand in a strawberry bowl and held a spoon with the other one. There were no clean spoons in the drawer, so she ate her cereal with a fork. The table was full of brown bottles, at least ten. Some of them stood up; some of them were lying down. They were all empty. On some of them there was a label. At school, Mrs. Gable told her to try to spell everything she read. Wendy loved Mrs. Gable. She focused on the label and started: J..I..M B..E..A..M, Jim Beam. When she was done eating the cereal, she drank her milk and washed the cup. She dried it and put it back in the cabinet.

As she walked toward her room, she noticed the basement door. It was shut, and that could only mean that Daddy wasn't going to see any patients today. The basement was his office and his operating room. On a normal day, at this hour in the morning, that door would be opened to welcome his patients. Since her mom had passed away, that door was seldom opened. Even when Daddy was down there for hours and hours—it happened very often these days—he would lock the door from the inside.

Then she went back to her room, combed her hair, brushed her teeth, and packed her pink backpack. She kissed Ben and went out to wait for the school bus. It was a beautiful day outside. The sky was a deep blue, still holding some shades from the previous night, and the air was cool and dry as she walked down the long gravel driveway to the road.

A few minutes later, a yellow bus stopped and the doors opened with a hiss. The driver had white hair and a large white mustache with two curls on either side of it.

"Good morning, Mr. Hindelman."

"Good morning, Miss; where's the doc?"

"He was feeling a little sick today."

Mr. Hindelman grunted in the way most adults did when they didn't believe what they were hearing, then smiled at her and said: "Jump in, princess, school's waiting."

She walked through the rows until she found a free seat at the very back. Her schoolmates were never enthusiastic when she sat near them. She had noticed some of the kids giggling behind her back at school. She didn't care that much, but she knew that they avoided her because of her daddy. She once heard two little girls—one of them was Linda Walker—talking about her drunk daddy. That had hurt. A week after listening to the false gossip, she had found Linda in the bathroom by herself, washing her hands. Wendy remembered how Linda had smiled at her, as if they were best friends all of a sudden. Wendy had grabbed her by the hair and slammed her head against the sink with all her strength. Then she left. Linda lost one of her teeth, and then the principal called Wendy into his office, where both of Linda's parents and Wendy's daddy waited with angry eyes.

So she had decided to limit interactions with the other kids.

Now, she sat alone, looking out the window as the bus restarted, hissing again. The curtains of her daddy's bedroom were still shut.

She hoped Ben would take care of him until she was back.

2

The school day went by fast, and when she jumped out of the bus and walked up the driveway, it was already 3:30 p.m. That afternoon, she was supposed to go see *Free Willy* at the theater with Daddy. Daddy had promised her. Rachel Mears—the only other kid she liked—was going, too, with her parents. The show was at five, but Wendy wanted to arrive a little early, so she and Daddy could get a large popcorn and two large sodas. Plus, Daddy loved to watch the trailers before the movie. That's why they always showed up twenty minutes in advance.

When she walked inside, the house was silent. The TV was off and the kitchen was still a mess, just like she had found it that morning. Wendy dropped her things in her room and said hi to Ben, who was still belly up on the bed, staring at the ceiling.

"Daddy?" Her voice echoed in the hallway.

No answer.

She walked to his bedroom. This time, the door was closed. She guessed that was a good sign; at least he had gotten up at some point. She grabbed the handle and turned the knob.

He was still in bed, but he wasn't sleeping. At least it didn't look like it.

He was laid out with only his underwear on, looking at the ceiling and trying to grasp something in the air. He panted and mumbled confused words, making garbled sounds, as if his mouth was paralyzed.

"Daddy, are you okay?" Her voice shook.

At the sound of her voice, his head turned suddenly toward her. His eyes were red and wide, as if he was terrified.

She screamed.

His focus abruptly shifted back to the ceiling. There was something he was trying to grasp in the air. But she couldn't see it.

"Jayne, mmh—mmh Jayne," he mumbled. "Give me my Jayne back."

"Daddy, who are you talking to?"

"*WHO ARE YOU?* Where's my Jayne," he cried to the ceiling. There was that darkness in his eyes. The shadow she had hoped he wouldn't have on this day. That obscurity, when he wasn't himself. He looked paralyzed. Only his head was able to move in sudden twitches. On the nightstand was a small jar with semi-transparent crystals in it.

Wendy closed the door and ran back to her room. She hugged Ben and cried, trying to catch her breath. When she had calmed down a little, she picked up the phone and called Rachel to tell her she couldn't make it to the theater because her daddy had a fever. Rachel was sad to hear that. Wendy told her she was sad, too, struggling not to cry.

When she hung up, she tried to focus and finish her homework.

After an hour or so, Daddy's bedroom door was still shut.

Wendy went into the kitchen and grabbed a frozen lasagna meal from the freezer. She put it into the microwave for three minutes, and then she ate it. The kitchen was dim and silent, lit only by the light on the stove. When she was done, she washed the plate and the silverware and filled up her glass of water in the sink.

Before going back to her bedroom, she went close to Daddy's door to hear if he had calmed down. She heard him snoring loudly. At least the delusions had passed, and he was resting. No shouts. Besides the snoring, the house was silent as if nobody lived there anymore.

Wendy opened the door and saw that Daddy was sleeping, covered in sweat. The room was hot and smelled awful. She put the glass down on the floor and opened his window slightly to let the fresh June air in. She got close to him and kissed him on his forehead, which was cold, very cold. His chest moved regularly back and forth. He looked better than he had before.

She didn't hate him, nor was she mad at him. She was just glad he was finally resting.

"I love you, Daddy," she whispered.

She went back to her room and wrote in her diary. It had a nice yellow fake leather cover. She wrote for almost an hour. Then she got ready to go to bed.

She set Ben in the bed with her, leaning the bear's head towards her so they could talk.

She could hear him saying: "*I'm sorry you didn't get to spend the day with him.*"

"I'm sorry too, Ben. But that's okay. There will be more days to celebrate."

"Are you scared, Wendy?"

"Yeah. I'm scared to lose my daddy."

Then she put herself underneath the blankets and turned the lights off. She didn't like the darkness. Things looked different at night. Everything was heavier then. Her daddy had taught her a trick to make things look better at night. She just had to close her eyes and breathe, counting four seconds each time before letting the air out. It usually worked, but usually daddy was there, counting for her.

It wasn't working now, but she kept trying all the same. She hugged Ben and she could hear her friend counting for her.

"I love you, Ben. Good night," she mumbled when her eyes started closing.

There was no answer to that. There was only a voice counting from a far place.

Five...four...three...two.

That was June 13th, and that was Wendy Jag's seventh birthday.

3

June 21, 2018

One... Wake up!

Wendy jerked her body upward, gasping for air, as reality reappeared all around her. For a split second, the air didn't get in and she felt like she was underwater. Her muscles didn't want to cooperate. Then, she could breathe again. The room around her looked tarnished, foggy. She saw yellow and white spots, produced by the light, glaring around the ceiling lamp. She looked around, and the room she was in didn't resemble her bedroom. Then the fog dissipated, and she remembered.

She wasn't seven anymore, and she wasn't in her bed hugging Ben. She was lying on a brown leather sofa. She was thirty-two years old, and a handsome man with green eyes and dark swept-back hair was sitting on a chair next to her. He had a notebook on his lap. He stared at her, compulsively taking notes.

"You're back," he said, smiling. "How are you feeling?" His voice was soft and warm as he handed her a glass of water.

She grabbed the glass and chugged the water in one breath, spilling some on her white blouse. Her throat was dry and sore. Her eyes were wide open with disbelief.

"The shock you're feeling is quite normal, especially after the first time," the man in the chair said.

"Huh?"

"Hypnosis is a powerful tool, Wendy. Do you feel comfortable sharing what you experienced with me?"

She realized with relief that he hadn't seen what she saw. He didn't know what she knew. She was still the only guardian of her memories. So she could administer little doses of her poisonous life to Dr. Murray. She wasn't ready to share more. Not at all. Giving out too much information was not good for her. She was aware of that fine line between truth and dramatization that she had to manage when she signed up for this. She was aware of therapist-patient confidentiality, but she wasn't sure the facts of her childhood would be covered by that.

"It was my birthday," she finally said in a raspy voice.

"That's good, that's really good." He kept taking notes. "What else can you remember?"

"Ben..."

"Who's Ben?"

"Uhm—Ben was my teddy bear."

Dr. Murray, who had surely been hoping to hear about some new person in her life—someone that could explain her anxiety or illuminate why this woman was so troubled—nodded, unable to hide a certain disappointment.

"Was it a happy day?" he asked.

"I went to the movies with my dad. We watched *Free Willy*."

"Is that the one with the killer whale?"

She nodded as a tear crossed her cheek.

"Is there any reason why you were crying during the hypnosis?"

Of course there is, she told herself, *my dad was an alcoholic, depressed, and addicted to ketamine. What else can we add to the list? Oh! Right. Should we talk about the basement, Dr. Murray? What about the little girl on the swing beneath the stars?*

"Honestly, not that I can think of." She held back and noticed Dr. Murray, always impeccable at not showing his emotions during therapy, sincerely disappointed. And she couldn't blame him. Quite honestly, she didn't understand how he wanted to keep her as a patient, after almost two years of refusing to disclose or share. Everything she had given out was always in minimal doses. She was also convinced that he proposed the hypnotherapy as a last resort before ditching her as a patient.

"Hmm." He closed the notebook and nudged his glasses up on his nose. "Listen, Wendy, I know we have agreed to do this with no rush, but I'm not going to be able to help you if we are not honest with each other. Do you understand that?"

"Yes. I do." She couldn't face him directly.

"Why did you come to me?"

"Because I cannot sleep."

"Right. And how do you think this works? Were you hoping for a prescription for drugs?"

She didn't respond and kept her gaze down.

"Wendy, do you want the easy solution or the real one?"

"I need to sleep, Dr. Murray."

He combed his hair back with his hand and sighed. He

stood up, moved behind his desk, and scribbled something on his prescription pad. Then he headed back to the sofa and kneeled. It almost looked like he was going to propose to her. She thought, in the delusive circumstance that she was a normal person, she could have said yes. Oh! That smile.

"Take one of these each night about an hour before bedtime. But before you do that, take a moment today and try to write down on a piece of paper what you remember of today's session. We will discuss it next Wednesday. Do we have a deal?"

She smiled back. She thought about her childhood diary and how easy it would have been to just hand it to him. He would have known what her world was made of. He would have known the darkness.

"Deal!"

4

One hour later, she walked through the front entrance of The Village, an apartment complex in the east suburbs of Albuquerque. She shared the usual circumstantial smiles—of all the social constraints, this was probably the one she hated the most—with her neighbors in the elevator. Then she rushed to her condo, number 721, and closed the door behind her just when she couldn't keep her composure anymore. She rested with her back against the door and cried. Eventually, she slid down until she sat on the soft carpet.

She had chosen The Village mainly out of convenience. It was cheap compared to other suburbs of Albuquerque. That had definitely helped her finances since selling the house she inherited in Copper City was out of the question. Copper City, the place where she was born and raised—if you could call her childhood a raising—was about an hour and a half away, driving east on the I-40. Close enough to allow her to go on the weekends when she couldn't resist the temptation, but not so close to tempt her to go there every day after work. Also, she worked as a dentist at a dental office in downtown Albuquerque, and she needed to be around. There were three other dentists working with her and sharing the building's lease. She didn't like any of them except for Rhonda.

Rhonda was the one who had noticed the early signs of sleep deprivation on Wendy's body: the bags underneath her eyes and how much weight she had lost. She asked if everything was okay, and she did it discreetly, which Wendy appreciated immensely. There was no judgment in her eyes. Rhonda said she knew a very good therapist, one who specialized in anxiety and sleep health. So Wendy didn't feel threatened when Rhonda passed her Dr. Murray's business card. Rhonda also confessed that she had been one of his patients and that he had helped her with her anxiety—so much that now she wasn't his patient anymore.

At first, Wendy didn't consider the possibility. Going to a shrink would be equal to admitting she was crazy. And she didn't think she was. People just didn't understand her. People didn't have a fucking clue, even though they acted like they knew. As if they had been through anything like what she'd had to go through. Not by a long shot.

So, she didn't go see Dr. Murray, but she kept the business card Rhonda had given her in her wallet, and sometimes, usually on Friday afternoons after work, she sat in her car crying and staring at it: *Dr. Clint Murray, Specialist in Hypnotherapy and Sleep Wellness.*

Fridays were her toughest days. Even though for most people, the weekend is the best part of the week, for her, the weekend meant free time. It meant that her mind was freer to wander. When her mind wandered, the troubles started. Part of her wished she could be forced to remain in her condo, meet people, and do what normal people do on a weekend. Read a book, go for a hike.

But the other half told her she had to go back to Copper City. Who would replace the flowers on Dad's grave? Who would keep the house tidy? And those were excuses mostly, she was aware of that, to justify her regular dose of self-punishment. As if it wasn't enough to have all those memories and nightmares in her mind. In that house, those memories were like a powerful magnet for dark thoughts. She could never get rid of them, not even with Dr. Murray's help.

In the last three years, she'd started to have these episodes of dismay followed by a sense of complete absence. They were not the worst thing she'd experienced, but they were unpleasant. She would wake up and wouldn't know how she ended up in that specific place. She wouldn't remember what she had done. The main reason she finally decided to see Dr. Murray, though, was the sleep deprivation. She knew she couldn't go on like this, with an average of two, three hours of sleep on a good day.

Today was her twenty-fourth session, and she still hadn't really told Dr. Murray anything. Not the important stuff, not the dark stuff, nor her episodes of absence. All she had revealed was that she needed something to help her relax and calm the anxiety.

And so she was on her way every Friday, driving back to Copper City. She had forced herself to accept it as a part of her routine. At first, the nightmares showed up only when she was in her old bed in Copper City, and they ceased when she was back in Albuquerque. That was back when she really thought she could see a way out. But now, no matter where she was, the nightmares followed her—from her childhood bed to her modern, coldly furnished condo.

And they were getting worse.

5

June 22, 2018

The next day was a Friday, and she finished her shift at 4:00 p.m. She drove to Copper City and, as always, she went straight to the cemetery. The graveyard was well-maintained, the grass freshly cut, the stones clean and polished. She was pleased to see that the fifty bucks she regularly gave to Ross Ferris—a local resident who tidied the graveyard to make some extra money—were serving their purpose and that her dad's tomb had the extra care it deserved.

On the white marbled stone with dark grey veining lay a red rose. A few dead and darkened petals had dropped. She replaced it with a fresh new flower. On the top part of the tombstone rested one of her old crayon drawings, made when she was a little girl. She had drawn herself and written Wendy underneath it. The girl held the hand of a tall, skinny man on the right, labeled Daddy. They both wore wide, semi-circular smiles. In the background, a woman stood as tall as Daddy. She had long, dark hair and she was all colored in black. Her mouth had been drawn open, as if she was screaming. The inside of her mouth was dark, and her eyes were two black circles on her wan face. In one hand, she held a bag full of teeth and in the other, a bag of money.

The letters written under this woman were thick, much thicker than on the other names. Wendy had pushed the crayon hard on the paper. Now, a gust of wind gave her a cold chill along her spine.

Beneath the woman was written: The Tooth Fairy.

6

After her visit to the graveyard, she drove home. The house was just outside of Copper City, about ten minutes away, in the hills. She parked in the gravel driveway and walked to the mailbox, where she used to wait for the bus every morning. Some days, Daddy was with her, holding her hands, kissing her forehead, saying he loved her before she jumped in. She would sit in the back and wave to him from the back window. He would stay there, waving back, until the bus was out of sight, down the hill. Some other days, especially near the end, he was in bed, and she was alone by the mailbox. But she would still look out from the back window with her hand gently laid onto the glass.

She stood there now, staring at the mailbox. She had refreshed the colors so that it would look like when she was a child. Nothing in the house had ever been moved. Everything had to look the same. She couldn't even begin to imagine what it would have been like to lose that last bit of memory and connection with the past. She had read a lot about grieving and absence and that it wasn't uncommon for people to see the dead, especially when the physical absence was too hard to accept. She didn't quite see her dad—she wished she could—but there was something around the house that awakened his presence inside her. It was like a gentle touch of wind, a whisper, a warm feeling on her skin. She could only feel it when she was around the house.

"Looks like there's a lot of mail for you," she said to no one, emptying the mailbox.

The mail was all for her. Grocery deals, coupons, a promo card with a picture of a fat man smiling with a thumbs up: *Injured in a wreck? Size doesn't matter, except the size of your settlement. Call Jerry, a lawyer to trust!*

She tossed everything in the trash can and went inside. The house smelled fresh, since she had set the timer on the air-conditioner the week before. For some reason the AC made her think about Oliver Burton.

On one occasion, a few years back, Mr. Burton, one of the neighbors—if that still applies to people living half mile away from the house—had driven by to drop a petition for Mayor Grebe. A dozen of the hill residents were asking the town hall to upgrade the sewage system, and Mr. Burton wondered if Wendy wanted to sign it. When he rang the bell four times and nobody opened, he had called to tell her that the AC was running and that the lights were on in the house. Mr. Burton knew that nobody lived in that house anymore, and Wendy's car wasn't in the driveway, so he was just making sure she didn't forget anything. When she answered the call, she had to use all her willpower not to tell him to fuck off and mind his own goddamn business. She limited herself to telling him not to worry, that she was at the grocery store, and she would be back soon. She also thanked him for the thought and told him to leave the petition in the mailbox. She was actually in Albuquerque at the time, and she wasn't planning to be back before the following weekend.

She knew a normal person would have turned everything off. She knew that. But that house wasn't normal. It was still a place of good memories, among the horrific ones. And she was determined to keep the house just as it was. Even if it was just so that she could live those brief moments whenever she wanted.

Who cared about the bills?

CHAPTER FOUR:

ANYWHERE BUT HERE!

1

June 24, 2018

W7th St. was just another road of many other thousands in the country. Four lanes—five, if you considered the one reserved for left turning—two for each direction, an uncountable number of junk food restaurants, gas stations, and billboards advertising insurance companies and lawyers specialized in car accidents ending up with injuries. Weren't those things what actually moved the country?

And so that road would have been just another anonymous one if it wasn't for the fact that, for some weird astral conjunction, the road also happened to be the old connection between Joplin, Missouri and Tulsa, Oklahoma, and it was also known as Old Route 66. That explained the unusual business of a lazy Sunday afternoon in the Midwest. No store would survive if it wasn't for that heavy number.

It must have been just past 1:00 p.m. when Jamal Anderson, or Jamie as everyone called him, dug in his pockets looking for coins. After some quick math, he calculated his fortune and concluded that it was roughly between two and three dollars. The special of the day at the Golden Fry Fish was fish and chips for two forty-five. The fact that the food had probably been fried in two-week-old oil didn't alarm him too much. Now wasn't the time to be picky, and any pretty decent amount of food was more than all right for him. On a relative scale, White Castle and Wendy's were places for white collars these days. Jamie's main worry now was about the sales tax. Man, with sales tax, you never knew.

So he decided to actually count his money while there was just one person in line in front of him. She was a bulky lady wearing too-tight yoga pants and flip flops. Her tank top was whiter than her pale skin. On her back, black printed letters read: *Go Big or Go Home.*

Judging from the massive fat rolls around her armpits, he guessed she had taken the advice a little too seriously.

"Can I get extra mustard and mayo? Thanks," she said loudly to the guy at the counter. He wore a blue-and-white striped cap with a yellow fish on the visor.

"Of course, ma'am. Can I get you anything else?" he asked in a high-pitched tone, faking a smile.

"That'll do it."

"Sure! It's going to be eight dollars and thirty-seven cents.

Would you like your receipt with you or in the bag?"

"Bag!"

"Thank you. Your food is going to be here before you blink. Can I help the next fried fish lover?"

By the time Jamal was called up to the counter, he had counted two dollars and seventy-four cents. So he knew it was going to be close.

"What can I get for you, sir?"

"I'll have today's special."

"Awesome, anything to drink?"

"Just some water."

"Absolutely. And will that be for here or to go?"

"For here," he said, knowing the possibility of getting back out in the ninety-five-degree-weather ashamed and hungry, was still a very concrete one.

"Excellent, sir. Your total is two seventy-two."

He tried to keep a certain decorum, but inside his chest there was a party going on. His stomach grumbled with gratitude. He emptied his right hand on the desk in a loud clattering of coins. The large woman was still there, standing to the side, observing the scene with interest. Jamie wondered if it was because he was broke or black. Or maybe both.

"Any sauce on the side?"

"No, that's fine, thanks."

"Would you like your receipt with you or in—"

The heavy hand of the woman landed on the counter with a metallic sound. When she lifted it, there was a quarter on the counter. The woman was staring straight into Jamie's eyes.

"How can you even think about having your fish and chips with no sauce? It would scratch the hell out of your throat when you swallow it, son. For Christ's sake! Show yourself some respect!"

2

When Jamie was done with his meal, he grabbed the backpack and loosened the belts that held his sleeping bag. He unzipped it and took out a leatherbound journal. The pages were made of yellowed, recycled paper which produced a nice antique look. It was the most valuable thing he owned, not only because it might contain the key, the only hope for a different life, but even more because Molly, his sister, had given it to him as a gift.

He could still remember the day when she handed it to him, wrapped in magazine papers. It was a relentlessly rainy night. Lightning and thunder were engaged in a gloomy battle. Outside, there was the deafening sound of the water hitting the metallic roofs of the trailers. The molded ceiling of their shared bedroom wasn't in great shape, so they had placed a bucket under the biggest leak. The regular clacking was driving Jamal insane.

"Jamie, this is for you. Happy birthday." She hugged him and shyly ran back to her bed, lying down on her stomach.

There was a pink card taped on the box. He could still remember the eight-year-old's handwriting:

Now you can write your story
On this journal so
When you'll be a famous writer
You can get me out of this place
Love you. Molly

And now, just as that night seven years ago, tears started gliding down his cheeks. He dried them with his arm, then smiled. "I'll get you out of there, Molly," he whispered. Truth was, he wasn't looking good these days. He had just used his last three dollars on shitty fried fish and chips. Not considering sidereal distance between him and Los Angeles. He was something like 1,500 miles away. Maybe more.

He packed his things and walked out. A surge of thick, hot air hit him right in the face. He crossed the street and sat in the shade of the Marathon gas station, next to the pump. Gas stations were the only places where he could fill his water bottle for free and, not secondarily, they offered shelter from the brutal sun in the midday hours. The heat was miserable and the air was heavy, filled with water; he struggled to pull it into his lungs. The heat on the asphalt distorted the road and the cars, confusing their shapes like in a mirage. He took a sip of cool water to rinse his mouth and poured some more on his neck and head. He put his Cleveland Cavs cap back on and walked toward the exit ramp. He fished a piece of cardboard from his backpack and held it at the height of his lap. The message on it had been true when he left Cleveland, and it was true now. He promised himself he would find a place where the cardboard's message wouldn't apply anymore. That would have been the place where he would have wanted to move Molly. The road had been exciting and adventurous, but it was tough and hostile, too. And the road was scary at night pretty much everywhere, especially where the neon buzzing street signs kept sending that merciless light down on the street.

He noticed a white minivan parked at the gas pump with a lady in the passenger seat, reading a magazine. In the back seat, two toddlers were rubbing their faces on the glass to make silly expressions. They waved at him. When he reciprocated, the lady turned back and yelled something to them, and then she rolled up the window on her side, looking nervously at the gas station entrance. He kept looking at her, not because he meant to intimidate her, but because he was fascinated by the way people try to avoid a gaze when they feel they are in danger. He got it, though; the lady didn't know him. And that was fine with him. A black guy on the edge of the road, wearing worn-out and discolored clothes, hitchhiking with a cardboard, saying "*Anywhere but here!*" didn't look like the safest thing for her family. He got that.

A guy in khaki shorts and a green striped golf shirt came out of the store. Jamie put him at about fifty. He jumped back in the car, the man looked on his left for the oncoming traffic, and eventually disappeared, mixing with the flow of the Route 66 travelers.

Two and a half hours later, Jamal was still there. The clock on one of the pump's digital screens read 4:07 pm. His luck for the day was draining out along with the water in his bottle—and what was left of it had quickly warmed. If it was tough to get a ride during the day, it was practically impossible at night—anyway, Jamie wasn't comfortable hitchhiking in the dark.

The sky was filled with big, uniform grey clouds, the color blending almost perfectly with that of the asphalt and the buildings, giving him the uncanny sense that he was stuck in a bowl of steam. The air was still, and even if the temperature had dropped a little as night fell, he couldn't feel any apparent benefit. His skin was sticky, and all he could think about was a bathtub with a cold beer on the edge of it. He knew he stank like a pile of sweaty crap, but that fact was at the bottom of his problem list.

He clutched his arms around his legs and rested his head between them, wondering how long he would have to wait on this street, collecting his last reserves of energy for another scary night. With any luck, he could beg for a few dollars to buy himself something to eat. He knew he would fall asleep at some point, even if he couldn't afford it. The road was different at night. Everything looked different at night.

The loud sound of an engine revving disrupted his thoughts. He turned and saw a green convertible parking at the pump. A tall, good-looking man with short curly hair and a large forehead jumped out and stretched his legs. His beard was at least a couple of weeks long. The man wore a dark blue t-shirt and a pair of jeans that were probably worth more than all the clothes Jamie had possessed in his whole lifespan. Jamie wouldn't have been surprised if the guy was an actor or a model; one of those dudes with enough testosterone to get a lady pregnant just by looking at her. Yeah, this guy was probably an actor, driving a fancy car that looked to belong in the 60s or 70s. It was dark green with white details, so well-kept and as shiny as if it had just come out of a car shop. The plaque on the front hood said it was a Jaguar.

What he felt at that moment had nothing to do with envy. It was just a pure, slow wave of sadness coming from the depths, flooding him with cold chills, despite the hellish temperature. The man turned his attention to Jamie, as if he sensed his gaze. Instinctively, Jamie diverted his glimpse like anyone would do if caught staring at someone.

"Hey, man. How's it going?" Mr. Curls said. He was arching his back and stretching his arms, so his voice carried a little strain.

Jamal raised his head and gave him a smile and a nod. Then he went back to his pose of self-pity.

"You alright, man?" the guy insisted. He took a few steps toward Jamie.

And that was the moment of uncontrollable outburst. Jamie didn't see it coming and didn't know why it happened in that exact moment—later on, he would think of it as the wheel of fortune turning finally back toward him—but he started crying. His eyes poured tears so violently that he could feel thick streams flowing down his cheeks, spilling onto his arms. He fell to his knees and hid his face in his hands. He tried to regain some sort of composure, but that uncontrollable way of letting himself go was still far from being over. He felt the man's hand on his shoulder, and only in that moment did he realize that he couldn't remember the last time someone had talked to him or treated him with such kindness, the last time someone had even asked how he was. Maybe that was the trigger: all the weight of indifference being taken away from him just by that simple question, in that simple moment.

"I'm good, man. I'm good. Sorry, I—I just had a moment."

"You sure did. You don't look too good, kid." The man offered his hand to help Jamie up.

Jamie grabbed his hand and stood, smiling, drying his tears with his palms.

"Let's get you something to drink; it's boiling out here."

3

Five minutes later they were standing next to the stranger's exotic car, clinking two very cold bottles of Boston lager. When Jamal took his first sip, it felt like a river had just flooded into a barren desert, filling all the cracks in his hoarse throat. He couldn't remember the last time he'd had a beer, but this one was the best of his life, no doubt. He enjoyed every second, every sip of that nectar and then tossed the bottle in the trash can.

The stranger pulled his credit card from the pump, chose the eighty-seven-octane fuel, and pushed the nozzle into the fuel tank. Considering all his time spent staring at roads, Jamal thought he had seen pretty much every kind of fancy car. But this one. This one was on a different level. It looked old—he could tell from the rims, the steering wheel, and the interior— but it was so well kept that it could have been one of those collection cars that really rich people keep in a garage all the time, riding in only for a couple of hours a week. One of the kind celebrities might have in their garage.

"I'm Johnny, by the way." The stranger broke the spell the car had put on Jamie.

"Jamal Anderson; people call me Jamie. Thanks for the beer, sir."

"Oh, please, cut the 'sir' crap," Johnny said, laughing. "Where are you from?"

"Cleveland, sir—ehm—Cleveland."

"That's a long way."

The twitch of the pump interrupted when Jamie was about to reply. Johnny hooked the nozzle back in the slot and had one long last sip of beer, then threw it in the trash.

"Where are you headed?"

Jamie showed him the cardboard sign. The man laughed.

"Well, I hear you, brother, and I don't blame you."

"Los Angeles," Jamie finally said.

"The man looked surprised and amused. "Los Angeles, huh? Isn't that a coincidence? I'm headed there too. Not exactly around the corner either. So, how exactly are you planning to get there?"

"Still working on it. Hitchhiking seems to be my only option right now."

Johnny laughed again. Then, he pulled his wallet out of his back pocket. He pulled out a fifty-dollar bill and offered it to Jamie.

Jamie shook his head, waving one hand in front of him.

"That's really kind, but I'm not asking for charity," he said. Deep inside, he wanted to take the money so badly. So far he had gone on using his savings only, but he knew that the time to ask for charity would soon come, without a job anyway. With fifty bucks, he could get a room and a shower. He knew he was going to regret this, but he couldn't take it.

"Go get us a six-pack, a pack of Marlboro Ultra-Lights, water, a Styrofoam cooler, and a bag of ice. We're going to need supplies for our trip to L.A."

Jamie stood there looking like an idiot for a few seconds, and then he grabbed the money. The man was smiling at him, looking genuinely amused. Jamie was walking towards the gas station when Johnny yelled at him.

"Hey, Jamie!"

Jamie turned.

"You come back with the wrong cigarettes and you'll have a long way to walk to L.A.," Johnny said and then laughed again.

As he walked into the store, he could feel the power of the money in his hands. It was a feeling that he suspected only folks who had scraped the bottom could understand. It wasn't his money, and he was very aware of that. But still, it gave him a sense of control, of safety and confidence. He had walked into this convenience store only a few hours before, afraid of being kicked out just for asking to fill his bottle of water. Now he walked in with fifty bucks to buy beer and cigarettes—and, most importantly, with the awareness that his plan to get to L.A. had just suddenly become more feasible, even realistic.

He got everything and walked out. The man was in the driver's seat, playing with the gas pedal. The six cylinders paid him back in a loud, impressive rumble of machinery that could only mean one thing: ready to go.

Jamie placed his bag in the small trunk. He noticed Johnny also had only a gym bag with him. Jamie placed the cooler with the beers underneath the passenger seat in between his feet. The seats were in matte red leather, so clean and taken care of that he felt bad sitting on them in his crappy clothes. Johnny didn't seem bothered.

"You ready?" he asked, plucking the pack of cigarettes from Jamal's front pocket. He lit one up, then offered the pack to Jamie. The kid grabbed one, took a couple of draws, and coughed.

"You know, I've never picked up a hitchhiker in my whole life. Should I trust you, Jamal Anderson? Wait, wasn't there a basketball player with that name?"

"Murray; he's still playing."

"Is that right? Well, let's see if we can make it to Los Angeles. You know? I was kinda getting bored traveling alone."

"I can't tell you how much I appreciate this. This is much more than I could ever have hoped for."

"Do you believe in destiny and all that stuff?"

"I don't. But I do believe in *karma*."

Johnny cruised the car toward the exit lane, then merged onto Old Route 66, heading west.

"Karma, huh? Like, do something good and something good will happen to you, and vice versa?" He ramped up the revs and used the long lever on his right to shift one gear up.

"Sounds about right."

"Well, it must not work for me, considering the pile of shit I've been through lately."

"Sorry to hear that."

Johnny didn't answer. He accelerated until he reached fifty miles per hour and cruised. The sun was getting bigger as it dropped down toward the horizon. The diffuse yellow light of the day's hottest hours was turning into a bloody orange. The clouds were shaded with purple and red. Jamie relaxed in the seat and closed his eyes, enjoying the warm wind on his skin. Somewhere in his subconscious, he was still waiting to wake up and find himself sitting on the concrete step of the gas station, hungry, thirsty, and scared.

But when he opened his eyes again, he was still in that fancy convertible car, resting his right arm on the door. An old song was playing on the radio. He wasn't sure of the title, but he was pretty damn sure it was by Led Zeppelin. It must have been.

The stranger and the hitchhiker rode west, facing the sun.

4

Later on, they would cross the Kansas state border, and after they passed through the little town of Galena, they'd travel into Oklahoma. Jamal wondered why the Old 66 traveled for such a short length in Kansas and then moved south into Oklahoma, rather than just reaching straight southwest and avoiding the double state line. Johnny answered he had no idea, but then he guessed it was because everyone wanted a slice of the cake.

Lots of folks would turn their heads as the pair of them passed through little towns, where time seemed to have stopped years ago. Old motels with their once-lively, now discolored walls, skeletons of old drive-ins and signs, standing there for the tourists like in a huge outdoor museum. Abandoned gas stations still showed their rusty vintage pumps. A concentration of melancholia from the old days gone.

Johnny suddenly slammed on the brakes and Jamie was caught by surprise. The tires shrieked on the hot asphalt. Then, he shifted into reverse and slowly backed up. He parked in front of a brick building and jumped out of the car. Beyond the third floor, on the roof, there was a huge white billboard reading: *Road does not end.*

Johnny's focus seemed to be on the house next to the building. Jamie turned to what Johnny was staring at. The walls were the color of rotten and damp wood. A gigantic red arrow had been painted on the side, white thick letters inviting travelers to stop here. It was a store and, according to the handwritten white cardboard, the name seemed to be Whitehall Mercantile: Collectibles and Antiques.

"Do you like old stuff?" Jamal asked, as he stared at the old house.

"I don't just like it. I love it."

"It's 7:00 p.m. The place must be closed," Jamie said.

"The OPEN sign is on. Let's check it out."

They were walking towards the patio when thunder rumbled in the distance. Jamal raised his eyes to the sky. Black clouds were moving in, fast. He could feel the air shifting, charging with humidity, crackling with static. The planks on the patio creaked under the visitors' weight. The shop's front window was a jumble of old license plates and memorabilia from the "mother" of all the roads. A large dreamcatcher hung in front of the red-painted door. Johnny stepped in and Jamal followed.

The store consisted of one big room, packed with all sorts of stuff. It was dark, and the air was spoiled. The smell of rotten wood was everywhere. There were many windows in the room, but they were so dusty that Jamie doubted the light could find its way in, even during the brightest hours. Two big chandeliers swayed on the ceiling, sending out a warm, feeble light.

The store was empty except for a lady staring at them from

behind the cashier's counter. Her hair was whiter than snow and she was so thin that a gust of wind could have blown her away. The thick, rectangular lenses of her glasses rested on the very tip of her nose. She stared at them in silence.

"Evening," Johnny greeted.

The woman didn't respond but reciprocated with a slight nod. Jamie could feel her eyes scrutinizing him. Johnny went straight to the "Sheet Music" section in the farthest corner, while Jamie took a look around, standing uneasy near the entrance. When he looked back at the woman at the counter, she wasn't looking anymore. She had returned to her sewing business.

Jamie grabbed his notebook and took some notes. On his right was a shelf holding all sorts of old dolls. They were neatly organized from the biggest to smallest ones. Some of them were dressed and in very good shape, while others were naked, missing an arm or an eye. One of them looked very well finished and lived in a glass shrine. It wore a red velvet dress. The black hair was neatly combed and covered by a Kentucky Derby hat. The porcelain skin was pale, and on her foot was a label written in what must have been Japanese or Chinese ideograms. Also, her features confirmed the doll's Asian origins.

Above the shelf with the dolls, on the wall, a large, framed painting hung slightly crooked. It depicted an unbridled white horse. Its body was half in light, half in darkness. A pale sun peeked from dark clouds, illuminating the back of the horse and the saddle only. The rider's lower body sat firmly on the saddle. The rider's body was missing from the waist up. It was dark and fascinating. Magnetic almost.

When Johnny put a hand on his shoulder, Jamie jumped but was also pleased he had done that. That painting had something beautifully wrong in it, and it had lulled him into a trance.

"Do you like it?" Johnny asked, looking at the painting, holding a vinyl record at his side.

"It's quite powerful," Jamie replied. "Creepy stuff."

"We'd better get going."

Jamie nodded and put his notebook back in his knapsack.

When they reached the front desk, Johnny cleared his throat, trying to get the old lady's attention. She gave a hint of a trembling smile. Slowly, she bent and hoisted an old, heavy book from underneath the desk. Her frail arms shook a little as she lifted the weight.

"Would you mind signing my visitor's book?" she asked.

"Of course." Johnny leafed through the pages.

"You have a beautiful smile, son."

"Thank you, ma'am. You are very kind."

"You know, this place was built in 1880, way before the Route. Always family owned. I've managed it since 1965. We like to keep track of the people who pass by."

Johnny saw that the last visitors that signed the book were a couple from Maryland: John and Missy Griffith. June 2007. That was eleven years ago. He didn't comment on that, and he signed the first empty row, then handed the pen—tied to the book with a piece of worn-out twine—to Jamie. He signed as well and pushed the book towards the lady, giving her a shy smile.

Johnny handed her the album he had picked from the shelf. It was *Route 66* by Nat King Cole: 12 inches, 33 rpm. A small label on the plastic wrap read "$10." He also laid down an Oklahoma license plate, with a similar handwritten label. The plate was fifteen bucks.

"Let me get a bag for you."

The operation took her about two minutes. Then she opened a tiny notebook she had on the desk. With the same hand that had written the prices on the labels, she wrote out a receipt and put Johnny's copy in the bag with the purchases.

"You have a wonderful day, sir." She smiled, handing him the brown paper bag.

"Thanks, ma'am. Would you recommend any hotel in the area?"

The lady took a few moments to think about it.

"My recommendation, son, is to drive as far as you can go from here."

5

Five minutes later, they were back on the road. The sky had turned dark, and at the horizon, Jamie could see a wall of rain coming their way. Johnny had closed the hard-top cover and turned on the headlights. The first drops landed like meteorites on the windshield with loud *plots*. Johnny put the wipers on full speed, but they couldn't keep up when the rain intensified. He slowed down, cruising the XKE at twenty miles per hour.

"Jesus Christ, it's coming down hard!" Jamie uttered, glad that he wasn't still at the gas station in Joplin.

"See if you can find us a place to stop for the night," Johnny said loudly, handing his phone to Jamie.

"There should be a motel a couple of miles ahead. La Quinta; it should be on the right. Does that sound okay?" Jamie asked. He was still a bit intimidated by Johnny and couldn't fully process the man's kindness. *If he's going to get a room for the night, I can't afford shit*, he thought. He could have slept in the car, but why in the world would Johnny leave him the keys? He was a goddamn hitchhiker on Route 66 for Christ's sake.

"Good. That's good," Johnny said.

As the world turned dark and the daylight trembled, close to extinction, the intensity of the rain reduced enough to let them see the green La Quinta sign a couple of hundred feet ahead.

Johnny parked underneath the canopy next to the reception and sighed. "That was pretty wild out there."

The parking lot was semi-deserted. A blue Chevy truck and an old Pontiac stood under the rain in front of one of the rooms on the ground floor. Johnny jumped out of the car and turned back to Jamie before stepping in the reception.

"I'll be right back. Relax; cigarettes are in the glove compartment."

Jamie knew where the cigarettes were. He also knew that his journey could end really soon. Johnny must have assumed he was broke in the moment he picked him up at the gas station in Joplin. During the brief conversation they had in the car, Jamie had the impression that money wasn't a source of concern for Johnny. Of course it wasn't. But was that enough to assume that Johnny would pay for his food, hotels, and so forth for the rest of the trip to L.A.? How could he pay him back?

He stepped out of the car and lit a Marlboro, resting his back on the racing-green door of the JKE. His mind was humming fast, filled with questions and doubts. Then he opened the door and grabbed his backpack, placing it on his left shoulder.

He debated whether he should leave a short message of gratitude to Johnny. He couldn't just walk away. It was still pouring rain. And where would he go?

But all the thoughts were interrupted when Johnny came out of the reception. He stopped at the entrance and stared at him. "What are you doing? Are you leaving?"

"Listen, man, I really appreciate what you're doing, but I don't think I can afford a motel room."

"So? Which one do you want: 217 or 218? I hate odd numbers, so I guess you'll take the 217."

"I'm not sure I can accept, Johnny. How am I going to pay you ba—"

"Go take a shower," Johnny interrupted him as he handed him the room key. "You stink, man."

6

Jamie shut the door of room 217 behind him and rested his back against it for a few moments. There were two queen size beds in the room. Four fluffy pillows were set on each bed. The walls were yellowish, and there were two wall-mounted lamps in between the beds. They released a soft warm light that filled the room. The AC unit was beneath the windows, covered by green curtains. The last time Jamie had slept in a bed was the week before. That had been more like a hostel than an actual motel. He'd had to share the room with six people, one of whom coughed all night long. The sheets were stained, and the room had smelled like an ashtray. It was better than the curb, but this? This felt like a goddamn Ritz-Carlton.

He dropped the knapsack on the floor and opened the door on his left to head for the bathroom when a heavy knock on the door made his heart sink in his chest. He opened without checking the peep hole. Johnny stood on the balcony holding a pile of clean clothes.

"Take these," he said. "You'll need them while you wash your other clothes. Don't need to return them to me. The laundry is on the first floor near the lobby. I ordered each of us a pizza. Yours will be delivered to your room."

"Why are you being so nice?" Jamie asked.

Johnny sighed and looked down, his face serious. Then he glanced back up at Jamie.

"Look, I'm just trying to help. We are going to the same place, right? Is it so weird for one person to help out another one?"

"It really is. I mean, not without a catch."

"There's no catch here. Just karma, if you want to call it that. Maybe one day this will turn out to be good for me in some way. Maybe not."

There was a subconscious kick in Jamie's gut that made him believe he could trust the man. He didn't know why or how. But he could trust him. He just needed the conscious part of him to realize it.

"I want to pay you back. I mean, not now. But eventually, I really want to."

"Alright. Fair enough, but don't think about it for now. Just get some rest. We've got a lot of roads to burn in the next few days." He grinned. "Good night, Jamie."

"Good night, Johnny," Jamie said and closed the door behind him.

He took his clothes off and placed them into a laundry bag that he found hanging in the closet. His first instinct was to toss them straight away—they were possibly too far gone anyway—but the road had taught him not to be wasteful. He turned on the faucet in the tub and looked at his naked reflection in the mirror while the steam started fogging it up. Then he jumped in and let the hot water hit his face. And man, it felt good. It felt so good that he stayed there for a half hour. Most likely the longest shower of his life. Soapy black water poured down the drain. But it felt good.

It felt as though he had just washed his soul clean.

7

After the shower, Jamie let his tired body land on the soft mattress. A wave of sadness crept in as the shadows lengthened in the room and old, scattered memories came to surface. The majority of them were not good. He sighed and thought, for a second, that this must have been a *Truman Show* kind of joke. Maybe it was the idea of escaping from his father, Ralph—a drunk who would only ever get up from the couch to grab another beer, yell at his mom (in the good days) and sustain the family by way of unemployment checks and stolen raw copper pipes for installations. Jamie's mom, Vanessa Anderson, used to tell Jamie all the time—even on Ralph's deathbed, in his last moments when he wasn't quite there anymore—that the best things his dad had made in his life were Molly and him. Jamie promised her that he would take care of both of them.

That's when the boulder of guilt always hit the hardest. He had failed in keeping that promise. How could he protect them by running away? But he knew he couldn't take them on the road before he figured out what this new life looked like, what the world out there looked like. So far, the world out there was worse than he had pictured. The sideral distances between people were astounding, an abyss between the souls.

But today, one of those souls had met his. It was still hard for Jamie to express that thought.

He grabbed his journal and sat with his legs crossed in front of him. There were days when he couldn't manage to put a goddamn word on the blank page. Other days, it all just came out like a flooded river. There weren't very many of those days, but today was one. His head was alive and the hand followed promptly. And then he knew once more he wanted to be a writer. It didn't matter if he would ever write a best-seller. Of course that was the dream. A more realistic short-term goal was to find a steady job that would give him the time and the peace of mind to write. He had a story, and he wanted to write it. A good story was no less than a boulder, a heavy raw block of marble. It was good because of its weight, but it would take time to sculpt it, to shape it, to make it his story.

He wrote for a couple of hours and then turned the iPod on, now finally charged. The sound of the Rolling Stones' piano filled the air in room 217, and Jamie slowly fell into a dreamless sleep on the notes of "She's a Rainbow."

CHAPTER FIVE:

KETAMINE

1

June 29th, 2018

Katy Donnington was fifty-five years old and lived with a hateful smirk constantly painted on her face. She was a gossip, always badmouthing someone. It was evident she got pleasure from it, that it fed her soul. On that particular Friday morning, she was blabbing about her neighbors, Janet and Thomas Barrymore, with particular focus on their nineteen-year-old daughter, who dressed like a whore.

"I once saw her getting in a car with two boys. God only knows what they were up to," she uttered while the anesthetic took possession of her upper gums. The last words came out slurred, as if she was drunk.

"We'll start in a few minutes. How are you feeling, Mrs. Donnington?" Wendy's smile was a gift she knew Mrs.

Donnington did not deserve.

"I feel like someone just punched me in the face. I guess that's how that spoiled brat would feel if she was my daughter," she burbled.

Wendy got her tools ready. She finished cleaning the towner scaler, which looked like a thin hook. On a separate tray, she prepared the mouth mirror, cotton pliers, and the Gracey curette.

Wendy reclined the back of the chair and raised it until she was comfortable enough to start.

"Open big," she said as she turned on the flat lamp on top of the main pole. Then she put the suction tool at the corner of her patient's mouth.

She didn't find a happy situation in her mouth, clinically speaking. She stared at a row of grey teeth with weakened enamel, rotting inside. The molar, the tooth that Mrs. Donnington had come in to have checked out, was the worst one, as the pulp was exposed.

"Any pain? Pressure?" she asked, gently touching the root with the tip of her hook. The slurping sound grew stronger as Mrs. Donnington started salivating. She shook her head.

Well, that's too bad, you cunt! Wendy thought. That thought and the hatred that came with it caught her by surprise. By the time her grin stretched her lips wide under the mask on her face, she knew that she wasn't Wendy anymore. She was something else—that something, which always came suddenly, with no notice or evident signs. It had been happening more often lately, and there wasn't much she could do besides observe it. Images flashed across her mind. There was blood, and there was pain, and there was pleasure. She was scared, but whatever took control of her in these moments was stronger than her fear.

The thought of the pain she could inflict on this horrible woman brushed her mind like a light breeze on a summer day. How vulnerable and fragile people could be when they offered their wide-open mouths to you. So trustful, so naive. She daydreamed of all the ways she could have killed Mrs. Donnington—or, even better, inflict pain. She could play with the root until the point when Mrs. Donnington would beg her to put an end to her useless life. That picture gave her pleasure, but she held it. Whatever took possession of her mind knew better, that it wouldn't be wise to do it here. Whatever that was, it knew there was a time for everything.

"Perfect. Let's begin," she said, sending those thoughts away.

But behind her surgical mask, the grin remained.

2

When she was done with the procedure and had filled a pain-killer prescription for Mrs. Donnington, there were no more patients for the day. She packed her things and left the dental office, with the intention to pay a visit to Dr. Murray. The darkness had vanished and she was herself again. *She* came and went as she pleased. There was a part of what was left of Wendy Jag that wanted help. But how could she find it? The reality was: the episodes had become more frequent since Dr. Murray had started digging in her subconscious, in those places where she didn't allow herself to wander.

The sun was still high and bright in the deep blue sky as she walked out of the building. The wind wafted the smell of New Mexico sand through the air. She walked to her car in the semi-deserted parking lot of the dental office. Fresh asphalt had been deposited recently and was still sticky under her heels. She threw her bag on the passenger seat and shut the door. Then, she turned the engine on and took a few deep breaths. When she looked in the rearview mirror, she noticed that her eyeliner had mixed with her unconscious tears and had started dribbling from the lower edge of her eyes.

She screamed.

Was *she* coming back? Why now? Or was *she* just making sure Wendy knew *she* was there, like a predator hidden in the jungle, ready to attack?

Wendy wailed, clinging to the steering wheel, crying out for help. A demand that no one could hear. She composed herself when she saw another car leaving the parking lot. She fixed her makeup and took a couple of deep breaths; then she headed to Dr. Murray's office.

3

Dr. Murray was looking at his phone when Wendy walked into the room. He wore a white linen shirt, which stood out nicely against his tanned skin. The sleeves were pulled up to just below the elbows. His eyes were blue, and his hair was neatly combed back. He was a very handsome man and, under different circumstances, she would have been glad to go on a date with him. She knew he was attracted to her. Despite his composure and professionalism, she could see the way he looked at her. So many men looked at her like that.

"Nice to see you, Wendy. Please,"—he gestured—"have a seat."

She shook his hand. His grip was solid. It made her feel fragile. Then she took a seat on the long leather couch.

"How have you been? Are you sleeping any better?"

"Yes," she confirmed. "I'm doing much better, and the medications are helping. I feel more focused at work, and the anxiety is going away."

Dr. Murray gave her a skeptical look and massaged his chin.

"Do you have something for me today?"

"Uh?"

"Did you write what I asked you to write?"

"Oh!" She rummaged nervously in her purse. Then she pulled out a yellow post-it note and handed it to him.

Dr. Murray looked intrigued. "Ketamine?"

She nodded, then put her purse on the floor and lay down.

"You told me to write down whatever I remembered from last session. My father was an addict. Among other things, he used ketamine."

He looked pleased. She'd known he would react like that. He wanted her to open up to him. There were many topics that couldn't be discussed, but she had to give him something, so ketamine was the sacrificial piece of truth.

"How about we skip the hypnosis this time and just dig deeper on this aspect?" He rested back on the chair. "Tell me more."

The idea of doing the talking and skipping the hypnosis disappointed her. She was starting to realize, deep inside her, the real reasons that pushed her to therapy.

"I think I could remember more this time. You know, with hypnosis. I think we should try it again. It was scary, but it also helped a lot." She tried to keep her voice calm, despite the fear that flared up in the back of her head.

He remained silent for a few moments, considering the idea.

"Wendy, I want you to be completely honest with me. You know hypnosis can be faked. Are you doing this just to get the pills?"

"I want to get better. The hypnosis was a shocking experience for me. I was scared the first time." That was true. She could still feel how vivid the memories had been. At home, she had tried to relax on her bed and do the same procedure to herself, but nothing had happened. There had been no slackening, no sounds, no images. Just far-off memories, small things. And darkness.

"Okay, then. Let's give it another try."

Her mind left the room quicker this time than she had before. She could still feel her chest moving up and down at a lazy pace. The dark wooden walls where Dr. Murray's graduations, certificates, and honors hung gradually blurred. A sense of drowsiness seized her and, in a matter of seconds, the numbers Dr. Murray was whispering became soft and perfectly blended with the sound of the unoccupied surrounding spaces of her subconscious. A place of imagination and madness, of silence and screams. She lost contact with the couch beneath her, and the void cradled her in a sweet lullaby.

Then everything faded to black.

4

December 20th, 1992

When she woke up, she was six years old. She looked out the window into the wide back yard and saw the guest house filled with Christmas lights. That was Edward Bowl's house. Technically, it was part of her dad's property, but Mr. Bowl had lived in it since she could remember.

Mr. Bowl was once a policeman, a detective. He had been

forced into early retirement after his wife died, because of the drinking. Wendy didn't know how that had happened, and her dad had ordered her to never ask Mr. Bowl. He was one of those men who needed a purpose in life. So, in his retirement, he volunteered at the dumpster, keeping it in order. He was also the guardian of the Jags' property. He worked as a handyman, gardener, and plumber. He was a pragmatic man, with more solutions than problems.

Several times, Wendy had seen him coming home from the dumpster with a piece of decent, brand-new furniture or an appliance that someone had thrown away. Old cathodic TVs, couches, recliners, coffee tables, sideboards, you name it. He refurbished them and sold them in backyard sales to the occasional tourist or traveler passing by. Tourists would buy anything. If you grabbed a turd and put a label on it saying that it was an antique piece of crap from the native Pueblos, they would hand over twenty bucks. Wendy got used to seeing Mr. Bowl around the house. He was a kind, silent, and hardworking man.

One day Wendy came back home from school and played with his bunny Roger for a while. Then she got tired and went back inside the house. A few hours later she went looking for Roger again, as it was time to feed it. When she couldn't find him in his cage, she went out in the back yard. Mr. Bowl was kneeling down with a shovel in his right hand. A fresh, small grave had been dug and covered back. Her dad stood there next to him, eyes down. He was sad, but he looked well. He was very different then than he had been in her last memory.

"Have you seen Roger?" she had asked in a trembling voice.

The two men had looked at each other, reluctant to speak. The doc took a deep breath and kneeled, clutching his daughter's arms.

"There was an accident, my love."

"What accident?" She knew already that something bad had happened. But the first touch of death in a young human life was a weird deal, a much simpler feeling of loss. A cold sense of emptiness landed on her chest, followed by incredulity. And she felt that sense of delay the body takes to process the disappearing of all connections. The real pain and the grief would come later, a few days after. Tears had drenched her pillow for many days and nights.

Until one day.

It was a sunny winter afternoon. The sun was cold and almost ready to plunge into the horizon, leaving the cloudless sky on the verge of turning purple. Wendy walked out from the back door and saw it.

On the far side of the yard, where the wooden fences demarcated the Jags' property, the bushes had been cut short except for one in the middle, which had been trimmed with mastery and art into the shape of a bunny. She walked toward it. A white piece of paper was secured to the bush with a twig, fluttering in the wind.

Nothing is forever,
Only who we are.

It wasn't signed, but she knew Mr. Bowl had left it for her. And her heart felt warm again.

5

March 17th, 1993

Memories followed one another in the melting pot of her subconscious. Dr. Murray's sofa was suspended in a dark, infinite room. His voice seemed to come from far away.

How about the ketamine? When did you find out?

She was yanked from the warmth of her last memory and thrown back in hell.

It was spring, she was still six years old, and she was having her afternoon snack in the kitchen. Peanut butter and jelly; her favorite. While chewing, she had noticed an odd movement in one of her teeth. She left her half-eaten sandwich on the counter and ran for Daddy. The fall of the first milk tooth had been the main topic in many of their discussions. Her favorite bedtime story was the one about the Tooth Fairy. And finally, she would get to be the main character.

Galvanized, she searched the house. She checked the office, the bedrooms, the front and back yards. *He must be in the basement*, she thought. That was the only place where she wasn't allowed to go.

99

Ever! No matter what.

She stood in front of the heavy metal door. A double deadbolt lock had been mounted on the side. The top lock was a chain door guard; at the bottom, there was a thick slide lock, which went more than two inches into the door frame. A long silver key was hung from the keyhole.

Her dad was down there.

A cold shudder crossed her back as she pulled the handle. The rusty hinges swung, filling the air with a squeak. Downstairs, the light was on. She could see the gleam on the green tiles. The air was soaked with the strong smell of fresh paint. Wendy hesitated at the doorstep, but she was too excited to wait. And it was a special occasion. The steps were silent under her light weight. She went down slowly, holding on to the handrail. She didn't know she wasn't breathing until her heart felt like exploding in her chest.

Going down there didn't seem like a great idea anymore. But she kept going.

When she reached the last step, she looked around. The workspace on the right side of the room was silent and dim. On the other side, the lamp on the desk was on. She couldn't see her dad. She thought about announcing herself, but the words wouldn't come out. Something on the desk had caught her attention. From that distance, it looked like a jar full of diamonds. She walked toward the desk, enraptured.

Next to the jar full of crystals was a plastic Ziplock with white powder inside and a vial. It looked like one of the medicines her dad used for his patients. Anesthetics, he had called them once. He had explained if he didn't use them, the patients would be in terrible pain during the procedures. It helped keep them calm.

And still.

The syringe on the desk dripped a slow tear on a piece of paper towel. She was about to grab the jar full of crystals when a voice came from her left, where the couch was standing in the dark.

"Wendy?"

The high-pitched scream that came out from her mouth was so loud it hurt her own ears. She ran to the stairs with her heart sinking in her chest. When she looked back and saw the tall, skinny figure of her dad, she stopped.

"Daddy?"

"What are you doing here? I thought I told you never to come down—"

"I'm sorry. But I have something to show you. It's really important."

Theodore Jag stepped forward from the darkness. The weak sunset's light filtered through the window and exposed his features. His face was hollowed from lack of sleep. Large bags had carved the outline of his eye sockets. Wendy didn't know about the withdrawal or the nightmares. She just thought he looked like he needed to eat something and get some rest.

"What is this about?" He came closer and kneeled in front of her, gently tucking her hair behind her ears.

She opened her mouth, trying to show the lower arch. Then she pointed to the incisor with her finger, touching it slightly to show him it was moving.

He smiled, amused.

"That's amazing, honey. Let me have a look," he said, taking his shaky hand to her mouth. It took him a couple of tries to grab the right one between the thumb and the pointer. Sure enough, he could feel the incisor getting loose in its pocket. "Go back upstairs and get some wire from out of the sewing box. You choose the color. I'll be upstairs in one hour."

"Is the Tooth Fairy going to come for me?"

"You can bet on it, darling. She will come for you. Now, go upstairs and never come back down here again without asking me first. Are we clear?"

"Yes, Daddy!" She hugged him and ran up the stairs, forgetting about everything she had seen on the desk. When she was halfway to the door, she turned and looked back down. Her dad was still kneeling and gazing at her. The smile on his face was broad but his eyes were wide open, almost panicked.

Wendy convinced herself to focus on the smile. Daddy was happy, and that made her happy. She climbed the remaining steps at incredible speed. Her fists were clenched with excitement. Every cell of her was focused on what color she would choose for the wire.

The Tooth Fairy will come for me, she thought.

6

Theodore Jag came upstairs a couple of hours later, around dinnertime. He found his daughter sitting at the kitchen table with the sewing box open. She had already picked out the purple wire thread. Before looping it around the milk tooth, he knelt and made sure the tooth was ready to come out. His hand was shaking, but he managed to feel the tooth. He wrapped and cut the wire, giving it enough length, and tied the other end to one of the chairs.

Just like Wendy had imagined it over and over in her mind, she closed her eyes and took two steps away from the chair. There was a gentle pressure on her tooth for a moment, and then the wire grabbed it and took it away.

She remained there with her mouth open, unable to contain her excitement. When she turned back to her dad, he had the wire in his hands, her small tooth hanging from it. He grabbed a circular mirror from one of the kitchen drawers and handed it to her, smiling.

Wendy looked at the empty slot in her mouth, then hugged her dad; then they prepared dinner.

Wendy ate her meal quickly, excited for what was next. She had her tooth safely shielded in a grey hanky, resting in the front pocket of her dress. Her hand incessantly touched the area around her pocket, to make sure it was still there. Daddy looked quiet as the night TV news went on.

"How was your day, Daddy?" she asked.

He jerked, as if he had been taken back from a dream. "Uh?"

"Did you have fun at work?"

"Oh! Yeah, yeah, it was fun. I had to get all my tools ready for a client tomorrow."

"Why do you have those diamonds on your desk?"

"Those aren't diamonds, sweetheart. That is a really powerful medicine that I use for my patients. It's dangerous. I never want you to touch it. Never! Promise me."

"I promise, Daddy."

"Like you promised not to come in the basement? That was a broken promise, you know that?"

"I'm sorry." She hung her head.

He scooted over and hugged her, kissing her on the forehead. "It's okay," he said. "Just don't go there anymore. There are dangerous things down there."

"What time will the Tooth Fairy come? I left a letter for her on the nightstand."

"I'm not sure. Let's get you ready for bed. Go brush your teeth; I'll be there in a few minutes."

She ran down the hallway and wore her pajamas. She waited for a time that seemed to never end. Eventually, she decided to jump out of bed and go look for Daddy.

While she walked down the hallway back toward the kitchen, she noticed that the basement's door was ajar, the usual weak light coming out of it. A cold chill ran up her spine when she heard noises coming from downstairs. She wanted to investigate, but she had vowed to keep her promise not even one hour ago.

Maybe he had gone to check if the Tooth Fairy had arrived. Would she come from the basement? Wendy didn't know. The only door was the one on top of the stairs. But Wendy knew that the Tooth Fairy was a magic creature. Anything was possible to her.

She heard a thumping sound coming from downstairs. She jumped out of her bed and, without thinking she was breaking her promise again, finding herself halfway down the stairs with her heart beating fast and cold drops of sweat running down her back. She ignored the voice in her mind that told her to go back to bed and went down a few more steps, just enough to have a clear visual of the room.

Light radiated from the small lamp on the desk, which sent long, trembling shadows all over the room. Daddy was standing still in front of the desk. If it wasn't for the shaking, Wendy might have thought that he was a statue.

She held her breath. She knew she mustn't be seen this time or she would be in real trouble.

Daddy grabbed some things from the drawer, then the bag of crystals. He started crushing them in a cup. Was he making a magic potion for the Tooth Fairy? Wendy wondered, excited. Her dad put the cup on the desk and bent over it.

Daddy made a loud snorting sound and launched his head backward, curving his back and staring at the ceiling. He had stopped shaking. He looked very still now.

He suddenly moved to the other side of the desk, and Wendy took one step back on the stair, feeling her heart in her throat. Daddy reached for one of the cabinets on the wall and took out a vial and a syringe, in a plastic wrap. When he had filled the syringe, he squirted it in a yellow cup that sat near his coffee machine.

Wendy slowly backed up the stairs and ran back to bed, making sure to leave the door ajar, exactly as she had found it.

When he finally made it to her room, ten minutes later, she was beneath the blankets with the nightstand lamp sending a spotlight down on the tiny incisor, which rested on a piece of paper towel. Next to it was a blue folded note: *For the Tooth Fairy from Wendy.*

"Are you ready for your big night?" he asked.

"I am!" she said, excited. "When will she come?"

"She will come when you are asleep. It will be dark in the room. She will find the tooth on your nightstand, and she will take it and replace it with a dollar bill. But there are some very important rules that you need to know first."

"What rules?"

"You know, she's very shy, and she doesn't like to be seen. If you look at her straight in the eyes, she will disappear."

"Okay, what else?"

"She wants you to be with no pajamas; it's a sign of trust for her. So you should sleep in your underwear."

She meditated on that for a bit, frowning. "Why's that?"

"I don't know, darling, but it won't work otherwise."

"Okay."

"The last rule is the most important. If you wake up and hear or feel something, you don't have to move. Don't scream, don't be scared. It will be her way of playing with you. It doesn't happen all the time, but if it does, you have to go along with it. Otherwise, she'll go away."

"Is she going to hurt me?"

"She won't. I will never let her hurt you. Okay?"

"Okay."

"Now, drink your milk and go to bed. Tomorrow you'll be a rich girl." He passed a hand over her hair, moving it off of her forehead.

She grabbed the yellow cup and drank it all. It had a bit of a bitter kick at the end. Then she took her pajamas off and pulled the blankets just below her chin.

"Good night, Daddy. I love you."

He was walking out of the room, but he stopped and turned back to her. "I love you too. Sleep well", she heard him saying while the world went black behind the sleeping mask.

He left the door ajar behind him.

Wendy stared at the darkness of her sleeping mask and took a deep breath. Then, the darkness became blurry, and in a matter of seconds she was asleep. After that, things got confused. She saw a woman with dark black hair and pale skin standing next to the bed. She couldn't tell if the woman had noticed her peeking. It all seemed like a dream. Wendy was cold and naked. But Daddy had told her not to wear her pajamas. She felt the touch of a heavy hand on her legs. She was scared, but Daddy had told her not to show her fear. He had said the Tooth Fairy wanted to play.

Then she screamed.

7

June 29th, 2018

The scream was so loud that Dr. Murray flinched in his chair. Then he reached out to her and put his hands on her shoulders and she stopped.

"Wendy. Is there anyone in the room?"

She mumbled something incomprehensible. He asked again as he observed the wrinkles on her forehead forming broad arches.

"Wendy. Who's in the room?"

"The Tooth Fairy; she wants to play..." she whispered

"What is she doing?"

"She's touching me. She wants to play." Her voice was a thin wisp. She didn't want to be heard.

Dr. Murray brought his fingers behind Wendy's ear and snapped them. At the same moment, Wendy opened her eyes. She was in tears.

"Welcome back, Wendy. How are you feeling?"

She didn't respond. It took her a few seconds to regain consciousness. She sat up abruptly, almost mechanically, as though someone had turned a switch on inside her. Her features were stuck in an unnatural smile. He found himself disturbed by the sight. The way she had woken up in tears and that grotesque persistent smile on her face now made chills creep down his spine.

"Wendy?"

She kept staring at him. Her face looked paralyzed. There was nothing in her eyes.

"Wendy? Can you hear me? You're back. Talk to me."

Her head snapped downward, and her hair covered her face. The gesture was so quick it didn't even seem human.

"I'm fine. Just a little confused. Can I have some water?"

He stood up and came back with a plastic glass.

"Wendy. Was the memory from before or after your mom died?"

"After."

She guzzled her water and exhaled deeply, still recovering.

"And when your mom died, you were only five, right?"

"That's right."

"Do you know if your dad dated any other women after your mom left?"

"He never had another woman," she answered irritably.

"Are you a hundred percent sure of that?"

"I'm fucking sure!"

He lingered there, looking at her with interested eyes. Then

109

he wrote something down, which irritated her even more.

"I have to go! I'm late." She rushed to grab her purse.

"Wendy, wait, please. Would you? Just a few seconds."

She stopped and stood there.

"I think this was a very positive session. The first one where I could actually get to know something about you. Don't you want to talk about it?"

"Talk about what doctor?" But she knew where he was going to. The part of her who had control now trembled, scared to know what he had sorted out.

"You said something about the Tooth Fairy. What does this mean to you?"

"Nothing. It's just a story I was scared about when I was a kid," she muttered irresolutely. "I really have to go. Can we move on from here next week?"

"Something's telling me you won't be back next week," he said with a sad half smile.

"I'll be here. I promise," she lied.

He took his prescription book and scribbled on it. "Here's your pills and something else I want you to start taking. Twice a day."

She took the prescription from his hands and walked away without looking back.

8

She stopped at the pharmacy. The lady at the drive-through window handed her a paper bag with two orange containers. The first one was the usual sleeping aid. The white label on the second bottle read: Lexapro 10 mg. She googled it and figured out that it was a potent antidepressant. She assailed the steering wheel, hitting it with all her strength until she hurt her hand. She hurled the container against the back seat and drove all the way to Copper City.

She didn't stop at the graveyard this time. When she approached the driveway, she left the car parked half on the gravel and half in the grass. She took a quick look around, to make sure nobody was in sight, then ran to the front door. When she shut it behind her, she leaned on it and took a few deep breaths. Still gasping for air, she rummaged in her purse for the heavy keychain that housed four long metallic keys and one small one. Each long key opened one of the four locks of the security door that led to the basement. The small key opened the white cabinet in the far end of the room.

Inside was a wooden red box, which looked like a carillon. She put it on the desk and opened it, pulling out a syringe and a vial, then pulled the plunger out to the 4 ml mark. She flicked the needle and a small tear came out of it. She laid it down on the desk and grabbed a rubber band from the drawer, gripping it around her left arm. She usually preferred to do it in the muscles, sometimes her calf, sometimes her deltoid. She had learned that the needle didn't leave any bruises or marks in the muscles. But this time she didn't care. This time she needed that a bit more.

When the vein had risen on the surface of her skin, she sank the needle into it. She pulled the plunger just a little, and a teardrop of blood spread into the transparent liquid, enchantingly crimson. Then she slowly pushed the plunger all the way in. Her eyelids trembled with pleasure and she loosened her grip on the rubber band as she leaned back in the chair. She rolled the chair into the middle of the room, where the summer sunset filtered through the window in a rectangular shape. Purple mixed with orange in the same ratio in which pain was mixed with pleasure. A thirty-four-year-old woman mixed with a six-year-old girl. Wendy mixed with the Tooth Fairy. And all of them mixed with the ghost of the abusive Daddy. *She wants to play, Wendy. She's very shy.* It was all mixed alright.

She will come for you.

And she played with her once more in her mind, gently hauled by that sense of lightness and blurriness. She played until the sun went down.

When the sun went down, though, things had changed. Because things were always worse at night. Things didn't look the same at night. They just weren't the same. When the night took over, the dreams stood the same chance as a bivouac during a storm.

After the sunset, there were only nightmares.

CHAPTER SIX:

ASK THE TOWN

1

June 30th, 2018

It must have been past 11:00 a.m. when Ross "Empty Bottle" Ferris tumbled on the hardwood floor at the El Dorado. Ryan Hesper sprayed beer from his mouth in loud laughter and got down from his stool to help him up. Even though it didn't take much to realize why people called him Empty Bottle, the folks in Copper City—especially the ones who hung out at the bar—could not realize how anyone could get to that level of drunkenness that early in the morning.

"Come on up, Ross! You old piece of junk," Ryan said, offering his hand to help him up. This level of drunkenness had become Ross's Saturday morning ritual. He liked to enjoy his time off, even if his sense of well-being usually ended just after lunch, when his body started disagreeing with the load of beer he'd managed to fill himself with.

"Get your goddamn hands off me," he yelled. Then he left twenty bucks on the bar and stumbled out of the place. He didn't own a car, and not purchasing one had probably been the wisest choice he'd ever made. He lived about half a mile away from the bar on the US-54, just outside downtown. The only three places he ever had to go were home, work, and the El Dorado—there he could be found almost every night lately and, of course, on Saturday mornings.

He worked at a copper mine in the great Robledo valley, as his father and his grandfather before him had. He rode there every day with Paul Bide, another Copper City fella, and they split the gas. It was an alright job, and he never complained about it. Every time someone told him how dangerous it could be for his health, he responded that copper was an essential element in the human body. Also, he felt very privileged, what with all the sci-fi shit miners had at their disposal these days, from super fancy oxygen masks to night vision goggles. His dad used to go down there with nothing more than a freaking bandana. Sometimes he wasn't even provided with a protective helmet. Not even a damn candle. Candles would have consumed all the oxygen down there and would have killed them.

The day was already as hot as hell. A very thin layer of mist made the sky look light grey, despite the burning sun being high in the sky. He had seen many summers in New Mexico—all the summers of his life, in fact—and this one had been hotter than usual. The sun rays were so intense that they seemed to literally run through you.

He was sweaty and drunk. The couch and his fan, at that moment, were just a mere illusion as the heat rising from the asphalt twisted the desert-like landscape around him. He tried to focus on the street. A white, rectangular sign in front of him proclaimed the forty-five-mile-per-hour speed limit. A white sedan hurtled by on his left. He didn't hear it coming, but he felt the air blow past him, almost knocking him out. He staggered to the edge of the road but managed to stay on his feet.

Five minutes later, he finally reached the shortcut: a side road that intersected US-54 and led straight to the state prison. He didn't like to use it, but it shortened the walk by pretty much ten minutes, so he went for it. It took him two minutes to cross the road. His head was spinning, and he felt dehydrated. *Isn't it funny*, he thought, *drinking like a goddamn fish and being dehydrated?* When he reached the other side of the road, he stumbled and fell face down in the ditch.

He groaned when a flash of pain invaded his right leg. *Please tell me it's not broken. I can't afford that*, he thought. He stayed there, lying under the sun, waiting for the pain to go away. The leg hurt, but he didn't think it was broken. That was a huge relief. He patted himself on the face, to loosen the dirt from his beard. Then he spat the sand out of his mouth. Somehow, he managed to raise himself and sit there. *Man, if I don't get my ass home, I'm going to kick the bucket right here*, he told himself. That thought scared him enough to put him back on his feet.

After a time, he finally saw the front porch of his house. His vision had gotten blurrier and darker than before. He felt his body was in a pretty bad situation, so he sped up the pace. He didn't go to the front door. That would have meant looking for the keys, unlocking the door. And he wasn't sure he had that time. He could pass out any minute now. So he went looking for the hose in the back yard. He was about six feet away from the red circular faucet when his legs collapsed. A cloud of sand and dirt rose in the air. He crawled with all the strength he had left.

His hand was now about two feet from the faucet. He screamed in pain as an intense cramp hit his right leg. He couldn't remember the last time he had any water.

One foot.

Finally, he managed to reach the faucet. When he tried to turn it, he realized his hands were too sweaty to grip it.

Goddammit, he thought as his head started spinning violently. He closed his eyes for a second and took a few deep breaths. He reached into the left pocket of his pants and yanked everything. A pack of Marlboro reds, a lighter, and a dozen coins came out. He dug deeper, and finally his numb fingers found the grey and white handkerchief. It was still damp with snot, but that didn't matter. He used it to get a better grip on the faucet. At first, it didn't budge, but he kept applying force and it finally turned. Not a lot, but enough.

There was a squealing noise in the water pipes. It was almost like a whine. Then the gurgle of the water followed. He grabbed the hose and pointed it straight to his mouth.

The water came strong. He felt the arid walls of his throat flood with water. At first the water was hot, as the hose had been under the sun the whole morning, but after a few seconds it went cold, and that was the most fulfilling drink of his life. He sent the water jet on his whole body, focusing particularly on his head, his neck, and his wrists. He could clearly feel the life coming back to him. He drank water until his stomach was sick and then he dragged himself to the shade, under the covered back patio.

He already had to pee, and that half gallon of water had made the situation worse. His legs weren't responding properly, and he was afraid he would fall back down if he tried to stand too early. So he let go and pissed his pants. He didn't even think about fighting it. He had already fought his battle for today. And he'd won. Too damn close this time. So he laughed as he felt the hot stream of his urine invading his waist and legs. He laughed hard. The water was still coming from the hose, and he had another mouthful.

Water comes in, water comes out, he thought and laughed even harder.

2

He woke up on the couch seven hours later. His throat was drier than sandpaper, his head throbbed like a drum, and his left arm had fallen asleep under his weight. He groaned and turned on his back. His arm tingled. He rummaged in his pocket and pulled out a shriveled pack of red Marlboros. He gave it a little shake and pulled one cigarette out with his lips. Then he lit it up, inhaling deeply.

He took a look at the clock on the wall: 7:15 p.m.

"Shit!" he muttered, spitting out the smoke. Outside, the sun was lying low at the horizon. He was supposed to do the cleaning at the graveyard. In fact, Theodore's Jag tombstone and surrounding area was supposed to be cleaned on Thursday. Every Friday the "hot dentist"—that's one of the nickname she had built for herself in town—came back to town, and the first thing she normally did was to go to the graveyard. She was giving him fifty bucks a week to do just that thing. *Just one goddamn thing, Ross, you drunk piece of shit.*

He sat upright on the couch and held his spinning head with both hands. He reached the already uncorked bottle of vodka on the stand next to the couch and took a sip. It burnt, all right. He took another long draw that almost burnt his lips. Then, he dropped the cigarette in a plastic bottle on the floor, half full of yellowish water with hundreds of other stumps. It stank like a thousand assholes.

"Alright, alright," he groaned, standing up. A fifty-dollar bill was a fifty-dollar bill. It was worth five hours of work at the mine. And that pretty face of President Grant. That motherfucker was tax-free. He walked from his back yard down to the dirt road toward the hill. The heat had diminished; a soft, tepid breeze blew from the west. That made the walk worthwhile. And the cash, of course.

Five minutes later, he reached the humble green graveyard gate. The fence wasn't taller than five feet and, for the majority of its length, it was rotting. It wasn't a great deterrent for people that had funny business in mind. But nobody in Copper City, not that he remembered anyway, had ever disrespected that place. Ross had the keys of the gate, as he also happened to be the graveyard's keeper. That wasn't an officially recognized role, as the town council didn't mean to have a keeper for the graveyard, probably because the town didn't have any money to pay for it. Ross had volunteered, and no one had challenged him, so he'd got the job. He was glad of that: it was an easy job, mowing the grass, pulling some weeds, sweeping the marble stones, and he got to visit his dad often. He didn't talk to him much when he was alive, but now they had a great deal of conversations about everything.

People left tips in the piggy bank box he had placed next to the entrance. That was also where the hot dentist, the old doc's—may his soul rest in peace—daughter, put the fifty bucks for the specific service on her father's tomb.

He reached the box and used a little key from his chain to unlock the lock that kept it closed. He opened the top and grabbed a handful of bills. There was the fifty and a few quarters. The rest was mainly pennies and dimes. He emptied it and put everything in his pocket, then lit another cigarette and walked into the graveyard.

The sun had fallen lower, and the light had shifted from

orange to purple. He rushed to the little barn where he kept his tools and the mower. The graveyard was his favorite place after his couch. Dead people that didn't talk much and he wasn't scared of them, but may he be damned if he was going to stay in a graveyard at night. And night was coming.

He turned on the mower and quickly trimmed the grass around one of the tombstones. The grass was already pretty tidy all around, but Wendy Jag wanted "special care" for her dad's stone, so he had to mow much more frequently than was really necessary. Then he put the mower back in the barn and ran to the other end of the field, where the crocus grew. He harvested about ten of them and cut the stems with his pocketknife to make them even. Then he went back to the stone and replaced the old flowers with the fresh ones.

He was cleaning dead petals off the stone when something caught his attention. At the base of the tombstone was a gleaming white object. It looked like a small pearl, lodged in a thin strip of fresh dirt.

He felt observed. He turned around. The breeze blew stronger for a moment, and he shivered. Nobody was around. He went back to the white object and pulled it out from the dirt.

"What the fuck..." he said. He could still see a few stains of blood mixed with the dirt on it. When he realized what it was, his first instinct was to retch.

It was a tooth.

The sun had almost disappeared behind the hills. Long

shadows started crawling on the tombstone. And again, that feeling of being observed. His heart rate had raised considerably. Okay, it was disgusting, but that wasn't the point. It felt terribly wrong, like an omen. One of those you can feel at the bottom of your spine. He pushed it back into the soil and left.

When he was halfway home, he felt more relaxed already. His heart had slowed back down. But his brain was still humming. Over the years, he had noticed other things on the stone. Drawings, letters, pictures. The hot dentist would always leave something for her father. On the rare occasion when they crossed paths at the graveyard, she would give him the money in advance for the next week's cleaning. Once, they almost had a conversation. Even though Ross was definitely thinking about her ass rather than listening to what she had to say, he could tell the loss of her father had hit her hard. There was a sort of absence in her eyes.

But this was sick. A chilling question took shape in his mind.

Whose tooth was that? It didn't even look rotten. Maybe one of her patients'? Maybe it was a fake. What did they call those? A capsule. That wouldn't explain the roots, the crumpled stripes of dead pulp. When his back yard was in sight, Ross took a deep breath, trying to push those thoughts away.

It had been a hell of a day.

3

July 1st, 2018

The early morning was quiet on the road. It had given Johnny some time to think, to recap. He had called his dad the night before to let him know he was okay and that the car was a blast. He hadn't made any contact with Ellen yet. He was surprised—and glad at the same time–to notice that the calls and the messages had reduced significantly. He didn't find more than one call or one text a day from her.

He took a few deep breaths, letting the cool, clean air of the morning fill his lungs.

"So you're a writer, huh?" Johnny put an end to what seemed an endless silence. Jamal had been quiet and thoughtful, his journal open on his lap. The pages fluttered as the wind invaded the cockpit. The radio was set unusually low.

The sun was already high in the clear, deep blue sky. White cotton balls were scattered in its vastness. The landscape was stunning. A triumph of colors was painted on the tiny mesas, celebrating the union of minerals and organic decaying materials. The air was warm and dry, pleasant on the skin. On the sides of the road the soil had turned from yellow to oxblood. Thick bushes, as tall as trees, were scattered over the golden hills.

"A wannabe for now. At least that's the plan," Jamie finally answered.

"Have you written anything so far?"

"A short story. And I'm working on my first novel now."

"Well, that makes you a writer, not a wannabe," Johnny said, smiling.

"I guess..." Jamie said, returning the smile.

"What do you write about?" Johnny asked. He winced with pain as he kept massaging his left cheek. He was worried that his tooth was getting worse.

"The genres I love to read are also the ones I love to write. I'm very much into dystopian fiction and horror stories." Jamal took a better look at his friend driving the car. "Are you okay? You don't look too good."

That was when the stabbing pain started. This time it was sudden and excruciating. The car swerved on the left, and the tires screeched. It all happened in a fraction of a second. A truck horn, coming from the opposite direction, blared hard. The second wave of pain was even worse than the first one. The pain radiated from his mouth straight into his brain. His right arm on the wheel felt numb, and his left hand was still pressed against his face. Then the car swerved back into the lane and the loud sound of the horn dissipated in the distance.

When he opened his eyes, he saw Jamie, with one hand on the wheel and the other one on the hand brake lever. He pulled hard and the car lost momentum. Eventually, they managed to pull the car over. Johnny was dripping with sweat, still holding the left side of his face.

"What the fuck, man. What's wrong?" Jamie asked, still panting.

Johnny jumped out of the car, and Jamie helped him walk over to the ditch. He was still holding on to his mouth with his left hand. He leaned forward and spit a mouthful of thick blood.

"Jesus Christ. We need to get you some help."

"Bring me the backpack. It's in the trunk," Johnny muttered.

Jamie left and came back with the green backpack.

"There should be some painkillers in the small pocket."

Jamie pulled out an orange bottle, opened the lid, and handed it to Johnny, then went to the car and came back with a bottle of water.

Johnny took the water and had a quick sip, then rinsed his mouth and spat again. Again, a mouthful of blood came out. He tossed three pills in his mouth and gulped water.

"I think something just exploded in my mouth. Must be that fucking tooth."

"We need to find a hospital."

"Hospital may be a little excessive, pal." He rinsed his mouth again.

"Let me find something. We can't keep driving with you in this condition."

Jamie went back to the car and grabbed his phone. There was barely any service in the area but just enough to let him open the Maps app and check their position.

"There's a little town twenty minutes west. Copper City.

There might be a dentist around there. If there isn't, we're halfway between Amarillo and Albuquerque. It's two and a half hours of road, each way."

"Fucking hell. We are in the middle of nowhere, aren't we?" Johnny muttered in dismay, trying to fight the pain.

"We could go back to Tucumcari, going east, but it's a forty-minute drive," Jamie continued.

"We don't go back, Jamie. We move forward. Get me to a dentist, before I pull this son of a bitch out of my mouth with my bare hands."

4

Copper City's main street was already quite crowded with its residents as the town prepared for the Fourth of July weekend. Fourth of July was always a good thing, if not for the patriotic spirit, then at least for the day off, the booze, and fireworks. But when it fell on a Wednesday, that wasn't just a good thing; it was an awesome thing, given the town and the residents could take a vacation bridge for Thursday and Friday, meaning a full five-day weekend.

On Main Street Mrs. Wallace was hanging a blue, red, and white circular bunting on the porch, singing softly to herself.

"What a gorgeous day, Edward, ain't it?" she said to the sharply dressed man passing by.

"It is indeed, Mary. Love your dress. Have a good day," Mr.

Bowl replied, hinting a bow and taking his hat off.

"Thank you! The same to you," she said, blushing.

He kept walking until he reached the corner on 2nd Street. Then, he stopped and took a look around. Hundreds of tiny flags fluttered in the warm wind coming from the west. The smell of grilled meat filled the air. The city was ready to start the festivities early this year. On the opposite side of the street, Allan River was proudly showing off the shiny sheriff badge hanging on his chest to the mayor, Oliver Grebe, and the other city council folks. It was an election year, and even though Mr. Bowl wasn't going to vote for Grebe's re-election, he had to admit the man had done a hell of a job with decorations and organization. On the other side of the street, a few stands had been set up to sell hamburgers, hot dogs, and cold beer. *Fat food, ugly decadence, and rigged games*, he thought. *It doesn't get much more American than this. Enjoy Copper City, folks, because after the weekend, God will forget it again.* He had seen it happen too many times to be fooled again. Undoubtedly the Fourth of July was that moment of the year when the town came alive. It was mainly because the tourists crowded the place in the high season. There wasn't any particular attraction for tourists in Copper City. The real attraction was the road that divided the town in half: the Old Route 66.

He hitched up his pants, which had been about the right size just two months ago, before that first fall. He'd been looking for varnish at Barney's, the local hardware store, when he had passed out, hitting his head heavily on the hardwood floor. He had woken up at the emergency room with a concussion. The only thing he clearly remembered was the smell of vomit on his shirt. Barney was with him in the hospital room when the doctor came with an x-ray sheet. He looked young, thirty-five. Forty at most. His hair was shiny, black as tar, neatly combed backward. He had placed the sheet on a square board hanging on the wall. Then he had flicked a switch on the side and the thing had turned on. On the left side of the x-ray sheet was a lateral view of his skull. He could see the shape of his head, the eye sockets and the nose cavity. On the right side were another four smaller x-ray pictures, all made from the top view of his head.

He glimpsed Barney's eyes and could see what sincere sorrow looked like. All things considered, it wasn't necessary to be a doctor to see what was going on in his head. It didn't matter from what angle you looked at the x-ray. A white object, probably the size of a grape, stood immersed in his skull. From the lateral view, Ed could see it just above the line of his ear. It was right in the middle of his head.

"Mr. Bowl, do you have a relative we can call for you?" the doctor asked.

He had shaken his head slowly.

"Any uncle, cousins, distant relat—"

"There is no one!" he said neatly. He was lying, of course, and that made him think of how long it had been since he'd heard from Diana. He had tried to call her every Sunday, but the phone kept ringing until he could hear her voice on the voicemail, once more. It was enough, he had realized in time, even just to hear her recorded voice. He had sent a few letters over the years, but they had all been returned. He kept them in a box in the hallway cabinet.

"Mr. Bowl, we have found a mass in your brain, and we reckon that was the reason you fainted." He fished a pen out of his white coat pocket and pointed it to the white spot on the x-ray sheet, right in the middle of Mr. Bowl's skull. "We will need to run more tests to understand what we're dealing with, but, judging from the shape and the contours, we think it is a glioblastoma." He said that last word quickly. Whatever it meant, it must have been pretty bad.

"How much time do I have left?" he asked, in a flat tone that surprised him, too. Barney cleared his throat.

"If it's what we believe it is, we are dealing with a pretty aggressive form of cancer. We need to run more tests to understand how advanced it is. Surgery is risky, given the location, but not impossible."

"How much time, doc?"

"With surgery, radiotherapy, and chemotherapy, eight to fifteen months." The doctor had finally sentenced. The answer gave Mr. Bowl no emotions, except for a little relief. At least it was more than a month or so. He had seen plenty of folks taken away in less than that.

And here he was, two months later and twenty pounds less, walking down the sidewalk on a beautiful summer day, letting the sun penetrate through his suit to kiss his skin. It felt good and made him smile.

Then he walked into El Dorado.

5

The place was packed with people. As he opened the door, a loud rattling of plates, hubbub of conversations, and the crying tantrums of spoiled kids assaulted him. The noise didn't bother him too much. It was good distraction, as he hadn't been out and about in town for a while–since the accident at the hardware shop. Everybody in town knew him, and they would all ask what happened, even though he was sure the word had spread quickly. A little confusion wouldn't do any harm.

In the background, hamburgers were hissing on the grill. Waiters were taking orders and delivering them at full speed. On the other side of the room, Roy Richard's son and three other fellas were getting the stand ready with their instruments. On the black bass drum, in white capital letters, was written the name of the band: *Say Your Prayers.* The dark hardwood floor was sticky under his feet, and God only knew how it would be at the end of the day. He spotted a free stool at the bar and walked there to claim it. He spotted Brett Burst waving at him. His face was a mix of relief and disbelief. Mr. Bowl waved back, then took his seat before anyone else could see him.

"Like a beer, Ed? Iced glass?" The bartender wore a starred

and striped undershirt that showed dark, thick hair on his chest sticking out from it.

"That'd be great, Steve, thank you."

He couldn't even take a full sip of his beer before Ross Ferris sat down at the free stool on his left.

"How's it going, Ed?" Ross's voice was unusually sober, given the hour in the afternoon.

"Good, Ross. Just trying to enjoy a beer," he muttered sarcastically.

"You son of a bitch! Where have you been?"

"Been quite busy with some stuff at home."

"Hey, listen. You worked at the Jags' for a long time. Isn't that right?" His tone was different. It might have been the sobriety, but it seemed more like Empty Bottle was frightened.

"That was a long time ago. Why do you ask?"

"You know I take care of the doc's grave every week? Right?"

He hadn't known that but nodded at him.

"Yesterday, I went up to the graveyard to take care of business as usual. Noticed something at the tombstone. I wasn't sure—it looked like a pebble, but it was too shiny." He paused for a second. "So, I checked it out."

"And?" Edward felt a glimmer of curiosity.

"The daughter, Ed. She goes there every week and always leaves something. And I don't nose around people's business. I just clean around the grave, keep it tidy. Throw the flowers away when they die."

"Make your point, Ross. I'm not quite following."

"It was a goddamn tooth, like the milk tooth children lose. What the hell? Now, I get it, leaving shit on your dad's grave. I've found drawings, necklaces, bracelets, all sorts of crap. But this—I don't know. It just creeps the shit out of me. I just felt like I had to tell you. I know you were close to the family."

As often happened, lately, the thought of Wendy Jag immediately connected in Mr. Bowl's head to thoughts of Diana. As a matter of fact, they didn't know each other. They hadn't grown up playing together in the neighborhood. There was a significant difference in age between them. Diana was fifteen years older than Wendy. When Diana left, Ed kept himself busy, burying his pain between the job at the Jags' and the dump. He couldn't quite explain how, but it felt fresh, selfishly diversionary, to be around a child that he hadn't failed. Wendy had a difficult childhood herself, and he had been there when she'd needed someone. Wendy had been his second chance, so he wasn't ashamed to consider her like a second daughter. They hadn't talked or seen one another. Not in the last four or five years.

He took a long sip of his beer. His hands got wet from the condensation on the glass. He thought he had never enjoyed a beer this much. Many simple moments in life had assumed a different meaning after his latest visit at the doctor.

"Thanks for letting me know," he said briefly. He kept watching the band. One of the guys was tuning a red and white Stratocaster, which took Edward back many years. He guzzled the rest of the beer and raised his right hand to the bartender to order another one.

"Like a beer, Ross?"

"I'll pass on that. Good to see you, Ed," he said and walked away without looking back. A burden weighed on the man; Edward could tell. He had lived in Copper City his whole life, and if there was something he hadn't seen yet, well, that was Empty Bottle refusing an offer of booze.

6

There are some places that seem to be collectors of bad stories. A magnet for evil feelings. Even the wealthiest, safest towns or neighborhoods have their secrets. But Copper City had always been a powerful conveyor of misfortunes. If Edward Bowl was ever asked how his life in Copper City had been, he would respond that it had been nice. He probably wouldn't mention that on a Tuesday evening after work, he had stopped to buy flowers for his wife—a small apology for years of mistakes-and then found her hanging from a beam. Her body still dangling in the stairwell, hitting the handrail, still moved by the momentum that had broken her neck just a few minutes before. He wouldn't tell you that it was too late to save her. He wouldn't tell you about when Diana came back home and found him crying and holding her mom's body, kissing the lifeless cheeks, which had become cool to the touch. He wouldn't tell you if you asked. But the town didn't need to ask. The town knew.

And if you asked Barney Hall how life had treated him, he

would say pretty fairly and he would be probably right. But he would deliberately forget to mention that a long time ago, when he was a still handsome twenty-three-year-old fella, he was driving back late at night, a little tipsy. He wouldn't tell you he had run over a Mexican guy on the country road, most likely an illegal immigrant trying to escape from his own hell, and that he had escaped scot free. If asked, he wouldn't mention that the man was still alive after the hit, that Barney had cleaned the front of his car all night long. The day after, it was in the newspaper, but no investigation had been opened. It was just an accident. That's how things worked in New Mexico back in the day, especially if you were an illegal immigrant. Barney would never speak of the nightmares that tormented him, every night of his life. The town would know that too. The town knew everything.

The town also knew why the old house that had been property of Harold Kenneth had been empty and on the market for more than four years. If asked, the town would tell you that a man suddenly lost his mind and massacred his whole family with a hammer and then took his own life twenty minutes later, standing on the rails with his arms wide open, welcoming the deadly hug of a train.

And what about the Jag family? The town didn't forget that either. What would Theodore Jag say, if he was still breathing air instead of worms? He would tell you he hadn't an easy life, but he wouldn't go into too much detail.

The town would tell you that Theodore Leonard Jag was born

in Lubbock, Texas, but he had lost the Texan attitude through the years, if he'd ever had one. He grew up in a Catholic family. His mom was all about church, and his dad was all about the flag and guns. Theodore liked it when his dad brought him to the hills to shoot at beer cans and bottles. But Rupert Jag's real passion was the booze, and that was the part Theodore didn't like. He would start after work with a six-pack and end up with cheap whiskey after the kids went to bed. The cigarette was always sticking between his fingers, while he rested on the chair in front of the TV. The ash was as long and lazy as his gaze, as he absently watched the night show. Sometimes Theodore would sit on the stairs and peek at the TV from the banister, always ready to run back to his room if he was caught, as he was supposed to be in bed by then.

The town would tell you that on one particular night, he sat there in his green jammies with polar bears all over, when his dad dropped the ashtray—full to the brim—on the carpet.

*"God dammit! Linda...*How many fucking times I have to tell you to empty this goddamn thing for Christ's sake?"

Linda Jag flinched while doing the dishes and dropped a plate in the kitchen. The pottery burst loudly into a thousand pieces.

"I am—I am so sorry," she stuttered with her heart jumping in her throat. She knew how the whiskey transformed her husband, and that night, the bottle was going down fast.

"You're a mess," he said, standing up in a flash. The movement was so sudden he almost lost his balance. He walked to her slowly with bloodshot eyes, breathing heavily with madness.

"How many times, Linda? Huh?" he asked, staring at her as he turned around the countertop.

"I'm so sorry, dear. Let me clean up my mess." She had seen him drunk so many times, but tonight he looked way past the limit. She turned her eyes down and moved to get the broom. He grabbed her arm firmly and pulled her to him. His breath smelled terrible, and his shirt was grey with ash. He stared at her as if he was meditating on whether to hit her or not. She couldn't face his eyes and sobbed silently. He turned her around and pushed her head on the counter. Then he bent and got close to her ear.

"You want to be silent now. Or the kid will hear. If you scream, he will wake up and come down. If he comes down, I'm going to hurt you. And then I am going to hurt him."

"Rupert, please." She wept as he pulled her panties down. He clamped his hand over her mouth and unzipped his pants. The screams were muffled by his hand and became quieter as she gave up, abandoning herself with absent eyes on the counter.

It was then that Theodore decided it was about time to go back to bed.

Still, the town would tell you there is more to the story.

Forty years later, a dispatcher redirected a 911 call to Copper City's sheriff. The call was made by a twelve-year-old girl named Wendy Jag, claiming there had been an accident at her house. The sheriff at that time was Tim Bourne, and he knew exactly who Wendy Jag was. The dentist's daughter. She went to school with his daughter Melissa.

When he arrived at the house, the front door was closed. Lights were off. He pulled his revolver out of the holster and placed the flashlight on the barrel. Then he turned the knob, and the door turned smoothly on its hinges. He walked in and found himself immersed in utter darkness.

He had been in that house many times, but this felt like the very first one. On his left, the kitchen was pitch black. The full moonlight washed the stairwell in silver. Something caught his attention at the top of the stairs.

A shadow.

He flinched and pointed the gun and the flashlight toward the movement. Sitting on the stairs was Wendy Jag, still in her school attire.

The sheriff took a moment to catch his breath.

"Wendy, sweetheart. Are you okay?" he asked. He patted on the wall in the dark, looking for the light switch. When he found it, he flicked it back and forth, but the big crystal chandelier hanging from the ceiling didn't turn on.

"Wendy! Are you hurt?" He pointed the flashlight at her. She kept staring in front of her, into an undefined spot in space.

"Wendy!" When he raised his voice, Wendy turned towards him.

"Are you hurt?"

She shook her head slowly.

"Where's your dad?"

She pointed her finger down as tears started to fill her eyes.

Her features stretched in a grimace of pure suffering. He tilted his head, then radioed: "Need immediate backup at the Jags'. Do you copy, Rick? Send an ambulance. The kid's in shock."

"Roger that, Sheriff, on our way. Over."

The sheriff turned back to the girl.

"Stay right there. I will be right back. Understand?" He realized his voice came out rough rather than comforting. She kept staring into the void.

He walked to the basement door, which had been left ajar. The keys were still hanging on the lock from the outside. A feeble light came from the metal door, left ajar. *Why so many locks, Doc?* He didn't recall so many of them the last time he was there. He had heard in town that the doc hadn't put any appointments in his schedule in the last three months. It all started to go down when his wife died. A slow but relentless downfall. The sheriff pulled the heavy door toward him.

The door squeaked on rusty hinges. The wooden steps were dusty, and the sheriff almost didn't recognize the basement's entrance where he had been several times. Where he had taken his wife and kids to take care of their teeth. The doc had always been maniacal with cleanliness. The pungent smell of ammonia and sterilized tools had gone away. He couldn't smell any of that. What he smelled now was completely different. Something his job had forced him to learn too many times. The unmistakable sweet smell of decay mixed with the ironic scent of blood.

He went down a couple of steps. The second one creaked under his weight, the only sound in a dreadful silence. It took the sheriff a couple more steps to realize he was actually frightened. And that wasn't something he was used to. Not anymore.

His left hand held the flashlight, which cast a trembling light beam. His right hand reached for his holster. He pointed the .45 down in front of him.

"Doc! Tim Bourne here; I'm coming down."

There was no answer.

He was three steps from the bottom when he was finally able to see the lamp, sitting on a solitary mahogany desk. From that distance, it seemed to him that the doc had fallen asleep on the chair behind it. His heart slowed down a bit.

"Theodore! Are you okay?" He stepped down from the last step, checking the blind spots on the other side of the room. The dental chairs and the tool table were covered with white sheets. The dust told him they hadn't been used for a while. When he was sure there was no one else in the room, he turned back to the desk, and that was when something on the floor captured his attention.

The shotgun's barrels gleamed softly in the feeble light, five or six inches below the doc's dangling hand. Tim put the pistol back in the holster and ran toward the desk. When he got there, he turned his head and took a few seconds to take some deep breaths. Then he turned back to the doc.

The left part of Theodore's face and skull had been spread on the wall behind him in a thick crimson spray. What was left of the other side would remain imprinted in the sheriff's memory for the rest of his life. He would see it randomly, closing the bathroom cabinet mirror after brushing his teeth on a Monday morning, or at church, on someone's face in the pew right behind him, or in a movie. He would squint, and that image would fade. But he knew in that first moment that sight was not going to abandon him. Not ever.

There was a noise coming from the stairs.

The twelve-year-old daughter of Theodore Jag stood on the third to last step.

"Jesus Christ!" he whispered; his voice was broken with sadness. He put the gun down. Her eyes were dark and empty. He could see that deep darkness even better in the dim light. And he knew right away that she would never be the same kid. The fragile strand that held things together, already weakened after her mom passed, had been broken beyond repair.

The noise of the front door slamming open came from upstairs. Lee Swob and Charlie Cliff called out. Wendy gazed impassively upstairs, and Tim came back to his senses.

"All clear. We are in the basement. Put the gun down. The kid is here with me. Send the coroner."

So... How were the Jags doing in Copper City? Ask the town. The town knew better.

The town knew everything.

CHAPTER SEVEN:

A CURE FOR THE SOUL

1

July 1st, 2018

The Jaguar came to a halt just in front of the El Dorado, about twenty feet from a small group of people chatting on the side of the road. One of them had to be the sheriff, Jamie thought, judging from the gleaming tin star on his chest. The tires screeched on the dirt and the engine stalled.

He glimpsed Johnny. He had a terribly wan look. The pain was eating him alive.

"Hold on a second," Jamie said from the driver's seat.

"Help, please. Has anyone got painkillers?" Jamie hollered.

Main Street fell in surreal silence. Everyone turned to look at him.

"For Christ's sake; my friend here is in a lot of pain. Please."

The bulky bald man with the sheriff's star on his chest rushed to the car.

"What happened, kid?" he asked.

"I'm not sure. I think one of his teeth exploded. He's bleeding from his mouth. We need something to calm the pain down. Then I'll take him to a dentist."

A man with thin white hair, wearing an elegant grey suit, joined them on the side of the car. He was tall and incredibly skinny.

"I may have something for him," he started off unflinchingly, then paused for a moment and stared at Jamie.

"Edward Bowl, by the way," he said and reached his hand out.

"Jamal Anderson." Jamie could feel the old man's bones under the dry and cold skin. His grip was strong.

"Is he allergic to any medications?"

"I'm not sure, sir."

The old man sighed, looked in the car, and saw Johnny barely able to keep his eyes open. His face was pearled with sweat. Mr. Bowl knew what pain was like. He shook four white circular pills into the palm of his hand. He took one and let the rest fall back in the bottle, then handed it to Johnny.

"Here, son. Take this."

Johnny desperately threw the pill in his mouth. He reached the bottle of water at his feet and took a sip. It felt like hot piss.

"What is that?" Jamie asked.

"Oxycodone," Mr. Bowl muttered, clamping the lid back on the bottle. "It'll knock him out."

"Thank you, Mr. Bowl; it's much appreciated."

"My pleasure, son, and please, call me Ed." The man looked back at the car. "Is this jewel yours?"

"It's my pal's. Well, actually, it's his dad's. He made me drive it just because he could barely keep his eyes open."

"You know, a lot of folks back in the day thought this was the most beautiful car ever made. I may be wrong, but I would bet this is a 1963. Am I right?"

"Honestly, sir, I've got no idea. You'll have to ask my friend."

Edward took a glance inside the car—where Johnny started to enjoy the wonders of Oxycodone—then back at Jamie. "When he wakes up, your friend owes me a ride in this beauty."

"I'm sure he'll give you one, sir."

Edward laughed.

"I'm afraid you won't find a dentist around here—I mean, not a proper dental facility. The closest one I can think of is the Dental Emergency in Albuquerque. That's quite a drive, though. But if you want to stop in town, I know someone that can help your friend."

"That would be great."

The people around them were slowly going back to their business and chats. The music had started at the El Dorado, and Sheriff River had gone back to brown-nosing the mayor and his friends at the town council. Folks flowed down the street, stopping at the souvenir stands, getting corn dogs and cotton candy. Edward Bowl gently closed the car's door and sighed.

"Like a beer, kid? You look like you could use a cold one."

"I should probably stay here. Check on him," Jamie said.

"The Oxy will knock him out good. He's not going anywhere."

2

Half an hour later, Jamal Anderson followed Mr. Bowl's old Chevy truck in the Jaguar. Johnny was still out on the passenger seat, his head bouncing at every bump along the road. Jamie glanced at him, feeling almost a sense of family. It didn't take long for the convenient company to transform into a friendship. That happened on rare occasions when people were on the same wavelength. And he couldn't be more grateful for it. Since he had met Johnny, his heart felt lighter, and so was the pen on the paper during the long days of driving. Several times, he had tried to learn more about Johnny's past, but he could never get much. He owned a tech company, something about computers and programming in Indianapolis. But something had happened. Jamie had deduced that whatever it was had something to do with Johnny's wife. He knew no more. The man had secrets, and Jamie knew when it was about time to stop asking.

Mr. Bowl took a hard left into a driveway. The tires screeched on the gravel. Jamie noticed a large aluminum silver mailbox. Crimson capital letters welcomed them into the property of Theodore and Wendy Jag. Jamie followed the cloud of dust raised by the truck, glad that the Jaguar's roof was closed. Along the driveway, a line of Italian cypress trees stood imposingly, screening off the strong rays of the afternoon sun.

Mr. Bowl stopped the car and got out, leaving the keys in the ignition. He rushed to the door and gestured at Jamie to wait in the car. The house was big, but it looked small with all the land surrounding it. The exterior was painted dark grey, and the windows' frames were black. It didn't look like a recent construction, but it looked well maintained. On the north side of the house, he saw part of what must have been a guest house, in the same color and style of the main property. There were no other cars besides the truck and the Jaguar.

From the driver's seat Jamie saw Mr. Bowl turning toward them from the front patio and shrugging. Then a movement from one of the windows caught Jamie's attention. He glimpsed the shape of a face peeking out from the tiny gap between the white curtains. The shape had black hair and the face was very pale. Jamie squinted through the dusty windshield.

The curtains were still and there was no gap between them.

The front door opened just a little, but Jamie couldn't tell who was on the other side from that angle. Mr. Bowl opened his arms wide. A long-legged woman in jean shorts ran out of the house and hugged him. They chatted a little, then she turned toward the Jaguar and nodded. Mr. Bowl gestured to get out of the car.

"Alright, buddy. Time to get out," Jamie said, shaking Johnny's shoulder.

"Alright—alright, man!" Johnny's voice sounded as if someone had just finished beating the crap out of him. His left cheek had swollen about twice as big as before.

Jamie got out of the car and went to the other side to help him out. When he offered to carry Johnny, the man refused. The prideful smile on his face was almost comical.

"Man, I'm high as fuck. This stuff is incredible." He started laughing.

"I'm glad you're having a good time, brother."

Johnny was about to reply when he saw the woman next to the old man; then he looked back at Jamie.

"Wow. You brought me to the woman of my dreams. The cure for my soul," he whispered

And Jamie couldn't blame him. The woman wore a sleeveless mahogany top, and dense chestnut brown hair was gathered in a braid. Her eyes were deep and dark. Darker than a moonless midnight sky. They were so full and so empty at the same time. Her lips were full and crimson, exalted by the pallor of her skin.

"How about we work on your mouth first?" the woman asked, blushing.

"Sorry, Wendy, you know how it is with Oxycodone. Please meet Jamal and Johnny. Folks, this is Wendy Jag. If her last name wasn't Jag, I would say she's my second daughter."

"Nice to meet you. I heard you had a little problem right there," she said, pointing at his face.

"Oh, yes. It hurts a lot," he managed to say.

"We can use my dad's old lab to take a look and see how bad it is." She turned to Edward. "Please, come in."

3

She led them into a big entrance hall, where light fell from the big window at the top of the stairs. She walked them into the living room.

"Lie down here," she said, smiling, pointing at the couch. Johnny wasn't sure if her smile was just a superficial one, but he believed she was attracted to him. He was a little rusty in the game of seduction. He hadn't played it in a long time, but some tools stored in dusty drawers in the back of the subconscious come out quickly when needed. In another drawer of his mind, not so dusty, his wife Ellen was still banging a masked man on their couch.

He kicked the thoughts out of his mind. The Oxy's effects were starting to fade away and the throbbing pain on its way back.

Wendy leaned forward, and for a moment, he thought she was going to kiss him. She turned on the lamp and took a black leather case out of her purse. She fished out a few silver tools, then put on an aseptic green mask, which made her eyes look even bigger and deeper.

"Open big," she said from behind the mask. Johnny couldn't

tell if she was still smiling. Her eyes were gelid and still.

He opened as she picked up a tool with a little circular mirror on one end. It was cold when she put it in his mouth. It clicked against his teeth. She pulled it out, and then she placed a plastic cup on the table in front of Johnny's face. He spat more blood than saliva. Then she was observing in his mouth with the mirror again. She put the tool down on the table and took off the mask.

"I'm not surprised that you're in so much pain. There is a bad infection in your gum. The bicuspid is damaged so badly that I can see the root."

"What can we do?" Jamal joined the conversation.

"Normally in these cases I would say to stay on antibiotics for a few days until the swelling reduces, and then we can treat the cavity. This infection is bad." She turned to Johnny. "How long have you been neglecting this?"

"A couple of months...I guess."

She sighed. "I have some antibiotics here. You need to start taking them immediately."

"Yes, boss."

"Is there any way you could treat the cavity too? I mean...I know it's unconventional, but what about the pain if the root stays like that?" Jamie asked.

"That's a good point," she said thoughtfully. "Between the exposed root and the abscess, you are going to be in a lot of pain. And I can't write a prescription for Oxycodone or Hydrocodone. Not if you're not my patient. I could be in trouble for that. How many more do you have?"

"We don't have any. Mr. Bowl was so kind as to give us a couple of his own."

Wendy's eyebrows arched with curiosity on her beautiful face. Edward Bowl sighed. His fists were clenched at his hips as he kept his face down.

"Brain tumor, Wendy. It doesn't look good."

"Edward, oh my—" She couldn't finish the sentence as tears filled her eyes.

"I have only another four or five pills until Tuesday. I don't know if those will be enough. Luckily I'm not taking them that much yet. Could you treat the cavity even with the swelling?"

It took a few moments to get back to herself. She dried the tears with her arm, then took a few deep breaths.

"With the gum so swollen and infected, there is a chance the anesthetic won't work." She was looking in the void, thinking out loud. "We would have to remove the tooth. The pain risk is still high, but more manageable." She turned back to Johnny. "If you don't care about losing the tooth, that'll do it."

Johnny realized she was even more beautiful than he had thought before. A slight pink had appeared on her cheeks. He couldn't tell if she was very vulnerable or very strong. His inability to read her made his spine tingle. It was an odd sensation. She was so beautiful and so uniquely cold.

"Rid the tooth, rid the pain," Johnny said.

4

While Wendy prepared for the procedure, the three men waited in the living room. Johnny and Jamie were on the couch, and Edward Bowl stood in front of them. His posture was straight and classy, his face an unflinching mask of composure as memories came to his mind. Everything in that house was the same. How many years had he spent around here, inside these walls? he thought, feeling the burden of the years on his shoulders.

Often, back in the days, he had overthought about time. He had been a detective in Albuquerque PD, homicide division. And that job changed the perception of time, to the point that he eventually had to stop thinking about it. He stopped because life fooled people, and it had fooled him all right. It fooled him into thinking that people gained some sort of wisdom and knowledge with time. The truth was that time doesn't teach anything. Time doesn't heal anything. It just loosens up the memories and increases delusions. Time didn't give him the wisdom to avoid the destruction of his family, even when he had the first signs right under his goddamn nose. And life didn't give him the time to fix the pain he had caused.

So here he was, reconnecting the dots in his mind, putting back together the shards of a part of his life that he had already started to forget. Nothing had much importance these days, but helping these guys in difficulty, seeing Wendy at the same time—after all this time—felt important. It gave him purpose.

"I'm sorry to hear you're not well." Jamie broke the train of Ed's thoughts.

"Don't be sorry, son!" His voice came out raspy, so he cleared his throat.

"How bad is it?" Johnny asked.

"Months. Maybe a year."

Nobody said anything. Ed was glad when he saw Wendy coming back in the room wearing a white gown. She announced she was ready for the procedure.

She walked towards the kitchen, and the others followed her to a heavy metallic door that led to the basement. Wendy went down first, then Johnny and Edward. The old man noticed all the padlocks hanging from the door frame. He followed the group downstairs. The smell of disinfectant invaded his nostrils. The furniture was old but clean. On the left was a solid desk with a laptop and a few yellow folders on it. On the ceiling were long rows of buzzing neon, shading a pale light on an old dental chair. She had put a nylon cloth on the chair, already reclined for the procedure. A long row of red and silver cabinets stood up against the wall.

"This place hasn't changed at all," Edward said with a nostalgic smile.

"I do my best to keep it. You know how protective of this place my dad was. It was his dungeon."

"So, your dad was a dentist, I guess?" Johnny joked.

"What makes you think that?" she asked with an ironic grin.

"Dentistry must have been a family calling then!"

"Or maybe a family curse," she said, laughing. Ed couldn't help but notice her tone didn't quite sound like her natural one.

5

When she finished preparing her tools, she turned to Johnny. Nothing about those eyes seemed real, Johnny thought. Looking at them was like staring into a black hole. Too deep to see the bottom, too strong not to be swallowed by it. For the following two hours, he watched her digging into his mouth. He tried to ignore the pressure of the needle sliding into his infected gum, the burning of the anesthetic shot, the buzzing sound of tools moving in and out of his mouth, the scratching sound of the hook on his teeth, the gurgling noise of the drool-sucking tool placed at the corner of his mouth. From that distance he couldn't tell if she was looking at him in the eyes. She wore a green surgical mask, and he was sure she was grinning behind it. He could tell from the delicate wrinkles at the corners of her eyes. And so he kept staring at those two burning black stars. The broken projector in his mind had stopped playing Ellen's movie, and now the film was going forward, projecting something new. Something he wasn't completely aware of yet.

When the time of the extraction came, she told him something, but he wasn't really listening. He nodded, unaware of what was going on around him. She clenched the tooth with her pincers and then pulled resolutely. He felt something cracking in the background of his numbed mouth. A fragment of tooth landed on his tongue. She pulled again and it came out. A warm liquid gushed out of his gum, tasting salty and metallic. It was blood. She placed a cotton swab onto the wound and told him to close his mouth and bite.

She sighed and pulled her mask down. Then she showed him the tooth, or at least what was left of it.

"No wonder you were in so much pain," she told him, analyzing the tooth as if it was a relic.

A few minutes later, he reopened his mouth, and when she removed the cotton, the wound had stopped bleeding. He grabbed the glass of water on his left, rinsed, and spat into the little sink that was part of the dental chair.

"Can I buy you a drink one of these days?" he asked, boldly.

"You know, drinks and antibiotics don't get along very well." She blushed.

6

When they left, Wendy waved goodbye from the porch. Mixed feelings were striking her, in the way a crush would strike a teenager. She tried to process those feelings quickly, to enjoy them fully, knowing that *she* could have come back at any time, erasing that sense of lightness in a blink. *Or* worse—and this thought scared her even more—*she* would let her enjoy the moment only to fulfil *her* own ultimate purposes. Wendy knew *she* was close. She had felt *her* for a brief moment while she was operating on Johnny's infection. Wendy was surprised to find herself smiling at the thought of Johnny, her heartbeat growing faster.

She went back inside and fixed a pot of coffee. She filled her mug and went back outside on the porch. She sat on the white rocking chair, willing herself to simply enjoy that view, that moment, that feeling. And so she did. She closed her eyes and let the sun kiss her skin, unthawing her soul. In a matter of seconds her breath became irregular, heavier. A whine came from the dark abysses of unexplored places. The mug trembled on the chair's arm. Her expression turned into a grimace, as if she'd tasted something rotten. *No, no, no; please. Please,* she begged in her mind, knowing what was coming.

From beneath the closed eyelids, the outline of the yellow bright light went darker, as if a cloud obscured the sun. The yellow became orange, then crimson, then purple. And she found herself resisting. Her fists clenched, and every muscle of her body flexed. And almost with the wonder that follows a magic trick, the purple went back to crimson, then to orange again. She took a few deep breaths, and her heart slowed down to normal. The whines turned to hisses then, just a slight wheeze. The twisted grimace on her lips disappeared, and the mug's clattering sound on the chair stopped, leaving only the sound of the breeze.

She opened her eyes and cried.

Rivulets crossed her cheeks, reaching the corners of her mouth, and she experienced that salty taste of freedom. She had won. She had clawed her way out to win that summer sunset. She sipped her coffee and smiled.

The air cooled down a little when the sun fell, reminding her that the night was coming. As the sun approached the horizon, the yellow light deepened. She saw it getting lower, corrupted by whatever was on the other side that stole its kindness. Far in the distance, wide clouds with vermillion, orange, and purple shades glowed over the horizon like merciless gemstones, indifferent to the darkness approaching.

That night, Wendy Jag slept in her bed with a smile on her face, giving herself the gift of a dreamless night.

7

Johnny woke up abruptly when the Jaguar came to a halt. His gum was sore, but the horrible pain was gone. And he was so glad for it. He turned to his left and saw Jamie, still a little rusty with the manual shifter, trying to put the car in neutral.

"How are you doing, pal?" Jamie asked.

Johnny groaned and sat up straight on the passenger seat. He passed a hand over his face to wake himself up and dry the drool that had poured from the side of his mouth.

"I'm good." He thought and paused. "Much better."

"I saw that. It seemed like you've never seen a gal before."

Jamie cackled.

"What are you talking about?"

"Wendy. You couldn't take your eyes off her."

"Well, that's pretty difficult to do when she's right on top of your face."

"Don't give me that shit." Jamie laughed. "But I have to say that it was a pretty bold move asking her out."

Johnny grinned at him before opening the passenger door and jumping out.

"What is this place?" he asked, looking at the house in front of him.

"Mr. Bowl offered for us to stay with him for the night. I supposed you were okay with that."

Johnny nodded, then turned his attention to Ed Bowl, who was still getting out of the old Chevy truck. The hinges squeaked when he slammed the door shut. He walked to the front door and fished out a heavy keychain from his jacket. Johnny could hear the clinking of the keys as his hand trembled. Then Ed bent over, aiming for the door lock. He walked in the darkness of the hall while Jamie and Johnny waited at the doorstep. The light went on, revealing a cozy living area in the warm glow of the nightstand lamp.

The first floor was one large, open space consisting of both the living room and the kitchen in the far end. The air was spoiled, and the shutters were down on the windows. There was a thin layer of dust on the coffee table in front of the couch. A white shirt and a pair of jeans rested on the chair. On the nightstand next to the lamp was a book with a pair of glasses laid across the warped cover. A black night robe hung untidily from one of the kitchen stools in front of the counter. The sink was heaped with dishes. A few TV dinner lasagna boxes rested on the stove.

"I'm sorry for the mess, gentlemen. I wasn't expecting to have visitors when I left home this morning. And I couldn't ask Sandra to come clean on the Fourth of July."

"This is perfect, Mr. Bowl. We can't thank you enough for the hospitality," Johnny said.

"It's not the Versailles' realms, but the guest room's bed is more comfortable than mine, and the coffee is fixed at least four times a day. Best you can find. Beans ground by yours truly. Quite a better deal than that Comfort Inn on I-40. Plus, I've got great news for you folks. I don't know why but I got too many hamburgers and beers yesterday at the market. There's food for ten people. The grill is going to be hot and the beers are going to be colder than freaking Antarctica. Please make yourself at home."

"That sounds like a dream, Mr. Bowl, " Jamie said.

"Oh, and please: stop that Mr. Bowl bullshit. Deal?"

"Deal!" they said in unison.

Edward tossed his jacket on the chair. The white shirt he was wearing was at least three sizes too big. The black belt was hooked to its last possible hole. There used to be a tall, broad guy in that suit, Johnny thought gloomily. Yet, the man still radiated a powerful and positive energy.

"Follow me. I still need to show you the best part," Edward said. He led them through the back door and they went outside.

As the night loomed, the diving sun had been reduced to a tiny red wedge. The back yard was wide and had a great view over the hills. The lights of Copper City went on, the Fourth of July's celebration ready to start. In the quiet of the hilltop they could still hear the music and the hollow bustle of the people flooding the streets.

Mr. Bowl appeared behind them with three bottles of La Cumbre. Lids already off.

"Not bad, huh?"

8

They ate hamburgers and drank beer. Mr. Bowl had lit a fire in a rusty brazier, filled with dry twigs. Edward Bowl thought that this might very likely be his last Fourth of July. And thinking of that gave him goosebumps, despite the warm evening wind. But he wasn't frightened. None of that was about fear. It was something different. It was more about awareness.

"Do you mind if I smoke, Ed?" Johnny asked with a hint of shame.

"Go for it. I guess you know that stuff is going to kill you."

He looked at Johnny nodding. He fished out a cigarette, then passed the pack to Jamie. They both took a long drag and exhaled. It was good to have people around. He couldn't remember the last time he had guests at his place.

Then Ed's attention shifted back to the crackling fire pit in front of him, which sent an enjoyable warmth to his legs. He loved the power that the fire had over him. It made him thoughtful, and it forcefully brought up all sorts of memories.

"Shouldn't we be telling stories around the fire?" Jamie asked.

"It depends on what kind of stories you want to tell or hear," Ed said.

"The kid likes stories. He writes them, actually," Johnny uttered.

"Is that right?" Edward asked.

"Uh-huh…" he muttered as he lit the cigarette, "something like that."

"What are these stories of yours about?" Ed's question came punctually.

"It's a dystopian novel," Jamie said briefly.

"What is it about all these people writing about the end of the world?"

"It's really not about the end of the world. It's more about what's after that. It's about the unique opportunity for humanity to reset itself in a new order. Let's say it's about second chances," Jamie said.

Mr. Bowl smiled. The passion burned inside the kid, and he could hear it loud and clear, like crackling twigs in a newborn fire.

"Alright, alright. Didn't mean to misinterpret you, Mr.

Anderson." He stood up stretched his back. "I think I'm going to bed. You gentlemen feel free to hang out as long as you want. Just don't set the house on fire."

He walked to the door and stopped by Johnny's chair. Then, with a surprisingly quick move, he offered him a handshake. Johnny felt there was something in Mr. Bowl's hand. The man kept staring at him with an odd grin on his face, shaking his hand, as if he wasn't sure if he should let go. Eventually he did, with a sigh.

"Good night, gentlemen," he finally said and went to bed.

"Good night, Ed," Jamie echoed, still staring at the fire.

When the back door shut behind him, Johnny opened his hand and found a piece of yellow paper, crumpled in a small ball. He flicked his cigarette in the ashtray and unfolded it. A sharp and neat handwriting appeared between the creases.

It was a phone number, and below the number was a name: Wendy.

He fished his phone out of his pocket and saved the number in his contacts. His mind was whirling with thoughts. Did she give the number to Mr. Bowl? Or was Mr. Bowl trying to set them up? He thought about sending her a text message right away, but then he remembered from the dusty drawers of his mind the most basic rule of dating: patience.

As they put out the fire, he felt alive for the first time in a long time, and the medicine for his soul was finally working. The broken projector's reels were slowly restarting after weeks of stillness. The tedious movie playing in his mind, which seemed hopelessly on pause, was eventually going to play again.

"What are you smiling about?" Jamie asked.

"The cure... I think it's working."

CHAPTER EIGHT:

SOMETHING'S BROKEN

1

July 3rd, 2018

It was a clear, warm night when Wendy came out of the bathroom. The alarm clock on the nightstand read 6:34 p.m. She stopped in front of the mirror and stared at herself. A white towel wrapped her body, partially covering her breasts but still showing her long pale legs. Her hair was still wet from the shower, and it fell on her shoulders in dark brown waves.

She bit her lower lip, as she did when she was nervous. Johnny would pick her up at 7:15 p.m. Two days had already passed since their first encounter, and she knew exactly where her anxiety was coming from.

Growing up, she never had any real desire to connect with other people at a sexual level. The sole idea of sex repulsed her. She had physical needs, of course, but she had always taken care of that by herself. Especially during college and dental school, she had tried repeatedly to date because she knew she should.

So she had dated many men—some of them very good-looking—but quickly realized she couldn't connect with any of them. She could barely remember their names. A few of them were not able to have an erection and blamed her for being absent and frigid.

So eventually, she stopped dating.

In the past year or so, though, something had changed. Something was bringing out a new sexuality in her.

On multiple occasions she had to repress the urge of asking Dr. Murray out during therapy. But then she thought about him a lot when it was time to take care of things by herself.

And now there was Johnny. Just the thought of him gave her an intense warmth between her legs. It frightened her because she knew she could not resist that kind of desire. She didn't want to resist. She knew she would have eventually let herself go completely with him, with no inhibitions.

That sense of impotence over *her* was growing at the same rhythm of her sexual desire for Johnny. This had nothing to do with love and romance. This was about bodies, skin and flesh. It was about odors and touch, chemistry and primordial instincts.

She let the towel fall on the floor. She looked at her body in the mirror and she knew right away that it was strongly trying to say something to her. Her breasts seemed slightly bigger than usual, and her nipples were turgid. She passed both her hands along her sides, down to the waist, and she felt pleasure from her own touch. Her skin was more sensitive than usual. Her body had become a capacitor, and she could feel the electricity from hair to toe, ready to explode.

So she was afraid, because she would have inevitably exposed herself. And she knew that, by exposing herself to her desire, she would become more vulnerable. She knew that the other side would find the gates wide open to come in.

To take over.

2

At 7:10 p.m., the Jaguar XKE turned into Wendy's driveway. The red, diffuse light of the evening glowed on the cypresses, giving Johnny the feeling he was driving in a dream. Like that time he and Ellen had gone to California and they'd driven along the Pacific Highway 1 in Big Sur, witnessing a stunning sunset. He kicked that thought into the back of his mind. He found himself trying to remember the last time he had gone on a date, and his mind inevitably brought him back to his first date with Ellen. On that time they danced all night long, losing perception of time and space. Everything else had disappeared around them; there was only her. How many things had changed since then? It felt like a long time ago; it felt like another life.

As the cypresses became sparser, he also remembered his inevitable tendency to commit, to rush things. He had tried to change that part of him with no success. The truth was that every time he was really attracted to someone, he could not just live the moment without picturing where that date or story might take him. This time was different, though. He was determined to just enjoy and live in the moment. *There's no shame in just wanting to sleep with her,* he told himself, looking at his glare in the rearview mirror, *and there's no fucking need to know what's going to happen tomorrow or the day after tomorrow.*

He stopped the car and looked at his phone: 7:14 p.m. Perfect timing. He jumped out and lit a cigarette while he waited. From down there he could see the only light that was on in the house—the room on the left on the second floor. He could see a silhouette of a body behind the curtain, probably projected by a table lamp. The shade seemed to be combing her hair. He couldn't help but picture himself in that room.

He kept staring at the window, and the shade seemed to vanish behind the yellow light when, with the corner of his eye, he perceived a movement on his right. In a room on the first floor of the house he saw the white curtain trembling. He walked toward the right side of the house with furrowed brows, but his phone vibrated in his pocket. It was Wendy, saying she would be ready in two minutes. He put his cigarette out, rubbing it under his boot's sole, and put the butt in the back pocket of his jeans. He realized his heart was thumping hard in his chest. His eyes fell on his left hand where he could clearly see the white gold wedding band resting for years on his ring finger. It had been there for over ten years. The finger and the ring, initially strangers, got acquainted with each other until the point they got used to one another and, eventually, ignored each other. He stared at the ring for a few seconds. Then he pulled the ring off and felt lighter. He felt free. He took a look inside the band, which read:

Johnny and Ellen Hawk, September 5th, 2009

He took a few steps back and flung the band with all the strength he had in his right arm. The ring disappeared from his sight and landed in the bushes.

The front door opened, and Wendy came out of it. She locked the door and walked toward the Jaguar.

"Well, Ms. Jag, may I say that you look stunning?" Johnny said as he walked to the other side of the car to open her door. And she did indeed. She wore a neat dark grey dress, which fell softly on her skin. Her hair was combed in a ponytail and her lipstick was as red as the sun, hiding behind the horizon at that very moment.

"You don't look too bad either, Mr. Hawk," Wendy said. She seemed slightly nervous. "That's a pretty neat car. Will you let me drive it?"

"We'll see. I don't even know you," Johnny teased her, gently patting the Jaguar and smiling back.

"Well, I think I'm going to surprise you," Wendy said, getting in the car. Her dress rode slightly up, discovering more of her legs. She didn't pull it down when she settled on the passenger seat. Johnny wondered if she had done it on purpose.

He gently shut her door and walked around the car.

"Where are we going?" she asked. Her dark eyes gleamed in the light. He could feel the electricity between them, so thick that it could have been sensed just by moving a finger through the air. So strong they could have been shocked just by touching each other's hands.

3

The Old Junction wasn't busy on that particular night, and Wendy was relieved to notice that. The less people who saw her having dinner with a stranger, the better. This was the classiest restaurant she knew not too far from town. She had never been there, but she had read about it. She was surprised that such a place could exist near Copper City.

Soft jazz filled the air, isolating their conversation from the rest of the room. Johnny had reserved the best table, which was more solitary than the others, in the farthest corner from the entrance.

"I remember telling you, very clearly, that you shouldn't drink while on antibiotics and painkillers," Wendy said as the waiter filled their glasses with the wine Johnny had picked up from the menu.

"Who said I'm taking them?" Johnny said, smiling as he raised his glass for a toast.

"So, how long will you be in Copper City?" Wendy asked.

"If you asked me a couple of days ago I would have probably said not for long. But I think I have a couple of reasons now to extend my stay. I'm sure Jamie won't mind."

"How did you guys meet anyway?"

"He was hitchhiking on the Old Route and I picked him up. Turns out we have a few things in common. We are both running away from something, looking for a fresh start."

"And what are you running away from?"

"You know, I've been asking myself that question for the whole trip, and every day I give myself a different answer. Maybe there are multiple things I'm running away from. A failed marriage, an unfulfilling job. I guess I'm just running away from the old me."

"Aren't we all?" she said, taking a sip of her wine. "Running away from something?"

"What about you? I have so many questions for you."

Wendy was worried that moment would come eventually.

"And what exactly do you want to know?" she asked, hoping he didn't notice the tremble in her voice.

"I don't know. What do you like to do in your free time? Hobbies, happy memories. Whatever you feel comfortable talking about."

The question struck her like a baseball bat in the face. Her whole thought flow shifted. She couldn't tell if that sudden reaction happened only in her mind or if her body was showing that too. She hoped Johnny couldn't tell. She didn't know what to tell him. The waiter came back for their order, and she had never been so glad to be interrupted.

She put her order in and asked directions for the ladies room, then excused herself and walked away from the table.

The restroom was empty, filled with the humming sound of the fans. She walked into one of the bathrooms and closed the door behind her. She sat on the toilet's lid and brought both her hands to her face, panting.

She was coming back and there wasn't much Wendy could do to avoid it this time. Every time she closed her eyes she could see *her*. Her breathing got more labored and her sight became blurry for a while.

Then everything went back to normal all of a sudden.

She was clearer than ever when she walked out of the bathroom and toward one of the sinks. She washed her hands and looked at herself in the mirror. She felt clearer and sharper than ever. She felt sexy too.

A young woman walked into the ladies room while Wendy admired herself in the mirror. The woman looked at her through the mirror.

"What the fuck are you looking at?" *she* asked.

The woman put her eyes down and quickly walked to one of the bathrooms, closing the door behind her.

She looked back at the mirror and grinned, and then *she* touched up her lipstick and headed back to the table.

"I ordered some small plates to share. Hope you don't mind," Johnny said, smiling. *She* had noticed he couldn't keep his eyes off *her*. And that was good.

"I sure don't mind. Where were we?" *she* asked, sensually biting her lower lip.

"Oh, sure! I was curious to hear something about the most attractive woman in Copper City. Her name is Wendy. You might have heard of her."

"Oh yeah! I think I know her. She doesn't like to talk much about her past because it wasn't a really happy one. She lost her mom too early. Before she passed, Wendy had promised her that she would have taken care of her daddy, that she would have become the woman of the house. Her dad was a dentist, as she is, but he was also an addict that ended up killing himself. That's all I know about Wendy's childhood."

Johnny's features had changed on the other side of the table. He cleared his voice and took a sip of his wine.

"I'm so sorry, Wendy, I didn't mean to—"

"It's okay, really. You told me that you are running away from your wife. This is what I'm running away from."

She took off one of her heels and started rubbing her foot against his leg.

"But I'm really glad we bumped into one another as we were running away."

"Ehm. Wow. I'm really glad too," he said, visibly excited. "I'm curious, though. Do you do this a lot? I mean dating?"

"Not really. There hasn't been anyone worth the trouble lately. What about you?"

"Absolutely not. It's been a long time since I dated someone.

I mean since my wife. I must look very rusty," he admitted, laughing.

"Maybe a little. So we need to make sure we take that rust off. Don't you think?"

"I think you're absolutely right. When do we start?" Johnny said.

"How about we go to my place so I can look at my schedule?"

4

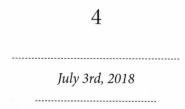

July 3rd, 2018

Thirty minutes later, the door at the Jags' residence banged violently open. Johnny slammed it back shut with the same passion as he lifted her against the wall. Their tongues danced with one another, and their hands were everywhere. She crossed her legs behind his back, and her moans became louder as she rushed through unbuttoning his shirt. His right hand was on her lower back and for the first time, he could feel the warmth of the soft skin that the dress had left uncovered. Something fell from the wall and crashed on the floor. But they didn't care. The surrounding world had become blurred, confused. In that parallel world the only space left was for the lovers.

Johnny's hand moved to her thighs, and he felt goosebumps

underneath his fingertips. He laid her on the floor and pulled her dress off, showing a perfect pair of breasts, which gleamed under the silver moonlight coming from the window. He kissed her neck at the base of her ears, and her moans sharpened. As she pulled off his pants, she felt the hardness of his passion and she kept kissing him until they were both naked under the silvery light. Her eyes looked different under the moonlight. They were not as defensive, as intimidating. They looked fragile. And even so, she had never been more beautiful and more magnetic than in that moment. In their moist and glistening pleasure, they became one. And again he couldn't look away from those eyes, as he witnessed the delight growing on her face. Their love didn't burn gently like a candle. Their love blazed like a fire in a forest. It raged with no compassion. And nobody could tame the fire of the lovers. One could only watch the sublime helplessly consuming itself until the deflagration.

Ultimately, the lovers' pleasure exploded at the same time. The flames, first fiery and tall, began to lose energy and became smaller, colder. The wind went weaker and the storm lost intensity, leaving a gentle breeze. The lovers lay on the floor, listening to one another's breath slowing down, gloomily watching the perfect storm moving away from them. The lovers know that the perfect storm was only one.

Somehow, in the deepest circle of their subconscious, they knew—it was never completely out of their minds—that whatever they had could not last for a very long time. And that reality felt as tough as the hardwood floor they lay on. They clung together in a sort of despairing sensuality, scavenging for the last crumbs of pleasure like two damned souls waiting for the clock to strike the end.

Then it was quiet again.

5

July 4th, 2018

The clock read 2:00 a.m., and she was still staring at him. He was peacefully sleeping in her childhood bed. Nobody had ever slept in her bed besides her, and she felt an uncomfortable sense of guilt. The white cotton linen rested softly on his naked body from the waist down. She kept staring at the neat curves that designed his chest and his abdomen.

He's so handsome, she thought, and for a moment she was tempted to jump on him and start all over again. Instead, she gently slipped out of the bed, being particularly careful not to put weight on the spot where she knew the mattress springs would squeak. She walked out of the room barefoot and left the door ajar. She sighed and gave him one last gaze.

Her breath had become heavier, and she knew why. Panic started flooding in her chest like water out of an open dam.

Aren't you the filthiest of the sluts?

The hideous voice came from deep inside her, so sudden that it made her flinch. She hadn't heard it for more than a day and, given the fact that the voice lived in her mind, that felt like a long time. It was strident, deep as thunder, and it didn't sound like anything belonging to this world. A wave of discouragement fell heavily over her. She knew this voice as accurately as she knew herself. *She* was livid, full of madness. Wendy didn't need to ask *her* why.

She ran down the stairs to the first floor, then climbed down another flight to the basement, making sure to lock the heavy door behind her. She knew there would be screams and, even if *she* was getting control again, the sane part of herself that remained didn't want Johnny to hear that madness.

What's wrong, little girl? Are you realizing what you have just done? You should've thought better. What in the world were you thinking? Now you've killed him...

This time, the voice was not in her mind. It came from Wendy's mouth, but it didn't sound like her at all. She was talking to a tall mirror, laid against the wall in front of her. Her head was tilted on the left side. The features of her face had shifted into an evil grimace. The eyes were wide open and an abhorrent, unnatural grin arose. It was the same grin she had seen in her dreams since that damned night.

"What do you want?" The words came out trembling in Wendy's voice.

That's wrong, my little filthy girl. What do YOU want?

"I want you to leave. Leave me alone," she muttered, and the soft voice seemed to disperse in the empty room.

Oh! Is that so? Do you REALLY want me to leave you?

Wendy kept her head down, incapable of looking at *her* in the mirror. Her heart galloped brutally in her chest. Wendy tried to respond, but nothing came out of her mouth.

I left you for a couple of days and look what you did. What would your dad think of his little girl, fucking a stranger like the worst of the whores? What would he say of the man sleeping in your bed right now? Do you want to know what he would say?

Wendy shook her head. A tear glided down her cheek.

"You didn't leave. You were there the whole time."

He would be disappointed. Is that what all his work was meant for? Perhaps he always knew you were a failure. Perhaps that's what pushed him to BLOW his brain UP against THAT WALL!

Wendy found herself pointing at the wall on her left. In the feeble light, she could see the shadow of the long shotgun barrels in her dad's mouth. Then she heard the deafening shot.

She fell on her knees with her hands pushing against her ears. When the room was silent again, she burst into tears. Her sobs were long and painful, yet hopelessly silent. They came from the agonized soul of someone who is ready to die.

You really think he loves you. Don't you? You really believe he's going to take care of you forever. Isn't that right, little girl?

"He might..."

NO, HE MIGHT NOT!

The voice came angrier than ever, so loud that she thought her eardrums were going to explode.

Now listen to me, you little shit. Do you want to redeem yourself?

On the verge of fainting, Wendy nodded weakly with her eyes closed.

You know what needs to be done. Don't you?

She nodded and began to cry again. In that moment Wendy knew that something in her was irreversibly broken. She didn't even try to fight. The decision had already been made. And from that point on, there was no way to go back.

"Something's broken," she whispered with her own voice in the silent room.

6

Daylight flooded the bedroom. A dry, gentle morning breeze moved the white linen curtains. With his eyes still closed, trying to keep the dreams with him a little longer, Johnny reached out, expecting to find her silk-smooth skin. The memories from the previous night began to come all together, and he smiled. *How did I live all these years without this?* He couldn't remember the last time he was intimate with Ellen—not in the mere sense of the word, but *this* intimate. How many times he had done it just to satisfy the crave of the body, leaving the soul starving for real pleasure. For the first time in a long time, he wasn't feeling any anger, any sense of guilt. He could even understand why Ellen had done what she had done. Both the body and the soul cannot survive without food, and they both refuse to die of starvation.

His hand didn't find anything but the soft white sheets. He turned and realized he was alone in bed. He stretched out with a satisfied yawn, then got up and dressed. He was about to step out of the room when a curious object caught his attention on the shelf that rested suspended above the childish writing desk. It was a brown teddy bear, which lay on his side in an unnatural position. On the front edge of the shelf, below it, was a sticky label, which read *Ben*.

"Hi, Ben," Johnny said, picking the bear up from the shelf. The bear looked at him through its glassy eyes. It was visibly old: the left ear was barely attached to the head, and its fur was not soft anymore. As he put it back in place, he noticed that all the other items on the shelf were dusty besides the bear, clean and dustless, and there was a journal.

Oh, come on, he told himself as he picked it up from the shelf, *you are not supposed to read someone else's diary*. He held it in his hands, passing a finger over the dust. It had a compass engraved on the front cover. A thin leather lace with an anchor hanging from the end of it was wrapped around the book to keep it closed. His heart sped up, aware of the violation. His ears were tuned to catch noises coming from downstairs. He breathed in deeply and, only partially ashamed of himself, he unwrapped the lace around the diary and opened it to a random page.

In the first part of the diary, the handwriting belonged to a kid—how old he couldn't exactly tell—until halfway through the diary. As he flipped quickly through the pages, the adult handwriting shifted from a rounded, childish style to a sharp-cornered and trembling one. The final letter of every word seemed to drag into the next one, almost like the pen had felt heavy and could not be lifted. But the most unusual thing was the strength that was used to keep the pen down to the paper. He could feel the words carved into the paper when he passed his finger over the page.

He kept flicking through. The nice and rounded style alternated with the sharp and dreadful one with surprising regularity. Without any conscious reason, he shivered and felt the utter silence of the house. He glanced in the direction of the door. Then he began to change pages slowly, almost as if it would have been a sacrilege to break the silence that had dropped all around him. His breathing became faster as he went to the final section of the diary and worked his way back through the blank pages, yellowed by the time, looking for the last recorded note.

When he found it, a sense of discomfort pervaded him. The last note Wendy had made was from today, July 4th. The page was filled with one sentence only, in the sweet, childish handwriting that he had found on the first part of the diary. He read it once more.

Something's broken.

7

He went downstairs, following the smell of coffee into the kitchen, which was empty. He saw a note on the kitchen counter, reading:

Went out running a few errands.
Have some coffee. Have you ever done it on a dental chair?
Wait for me in the basement.
Will be back soon. Happy 4th *of July.*
P.S. I hope you don't mind I took your fancy car.

He put the note down and smiled. It occurred to him to think that the whole situation felt already a little like a marriage. In the back of his mind there was still the diary. He stopped wondering what that final sentence could have meant, but he had noticed that the handwriting on the yellow paper was different from both the handwritings he had found in the diary.

He poured himself some coffee in a tall, dark red mug. The coffee had a little bit of a bitter kick at the end, but as his dad used to say all the time: *I've paid for worse and got better ones for free.*

It struck him again how silent the house was. He couldn't hear a single background noise, not a bird singing outside, no cars passing by in the distance. A thought kept crawling unpleasantly in the back of his mind: why would she take my car? Not that he really cared, but wasn't she concerned about being seen around with his car? He couldn't say that he knew Wendy very well, but she seemed quite a private woman, not the kind who liked to be the talk of the small town. She had told him clearly, the night before at dinner, that she hated Copper City for all the gossip. He could already picture the old folks, talking at the bar, bad mouthing about her.

He took another sip and walked through the narrow hallway, which led to the garage. The mug was hot in the palm of his hand. His eye fell on the heavy door that led to the basement. The padlocks were unlocked, and a keychain with a long key hung lifelessly from the main lock.

He turned the handle and the door answered with a long squeaking sound.

He ventured cautiously down the stairs. The planks creaked under the weight of his steps. The basement was cooler than it had been a few days before. He walked around, recognizing the dentist chair where he'd been lying as Wendy had worked on his tooth. The thought of having a second round on that chair sounded really hot to him.

On the right side of the room, where the dentist's chair was placed, the walls and the floor were covered with green tiles. Behind the chair was an old futon, hidden on the darkest side of the basement. On the longest wall, just behind the staircase, there was a long rank of file cabinets. They must have contained all the dental history of Copper City. On the other side of the room was a large wooden desk, which looked incredibly sturdy and heavy. The side that was facing him had a recess, which transformed it into a bookshelf. The books were mainly about dentistry and orthodontics techniques. They looked old and dusty. They must have belonged to Wendy's father.

He went around the desk, resting his arms on the back of the black leather chair, and took a long sip of coffee, which had begun to reach a more acceptable temperature. For a moment, the world seemed to spin all around him. He closed his eyes, and that made it even worse. He took another sip of coffee and straightened himself back up, and he flinched when he opened his eyes again. The shadows produced by the light flooding from the narrow windows in the basement had changed. The dizziness got stronger, and he started to feel weak. Cold drops of sweat beaded his forehead. A long dark shadow had appeared right in front of him, elongated by the light coming from...

Behind me. Someone's behind me, he thought.

When he turned, a dreadful sense of terror spread inside him down to the bones. His first instinct was to put his hands in front of his face, to hide from his sight the ghastly shape that stood in front of him. He fell heavily on his back as he tried to move away. The mug shattered on the floor. His head was spinning more than ever. He felt like passing out, but the adrenaline running in his body kept him awake. He squinted, childishly hoping that it was all a dream. But *she* was still there, standing still with her head tilted at an unnatural angle.

A thick layer of long black hair covered her face. She stood perfectly still in a white robe two or three sizes bigger than her body. Then he realized that wasn't her face. She was wearing some sort of Halloween mask. It was wan with dark holes for the eyes, some sort of creepy wax mask.

"Ah ah ah. Very funny," he said, relieved. "You got me there. Jeez, where did you find that mask?" His head was spinning like crazy.

She didn't move one inch.

"Wendy? Is this some kind of joke?" Johnny's voice came out choked, soaked in fear. His head was a vortex of blurry images mixed with darkness. He gasped, hungry for air.

She began to walk very slowly in his direction.

He backed up on his bottom, crawling on the cold, polished floor. The effort that it took for him to move twenty inches felt the same as running three miles and, all at once, he felt incredibly cold. He was going to die.

What the fuck is happening? Johnny asked whatever was left of his mind. *Am I dying? Why do I feel so sick?*

The coffee, the fucking coffee, he thought, *is drugged.*

When the ominous figure in front of him stepped forward again, the long dark hair waved, showing a dreadful grin.

His strength abandoned him. His elbows felt numb and when his arms surrendered, he landed on his back, staring at the ceiling. He could feel his heart slowing down. Then she was on top of him, and even though the world was getting dark around him, he could see that the thick black hair was not real. *It's a wig,* he thought, *and that grin. That grin is not real.* Then the ceiling went dark and brought all the world away from him.

8

The Tooth Fairy takes
But she gives in return.
An honest trade with no guessing.
A trophy you just have to earn...

He had been in and out for hours, falling asleep and waking back up to the same nightmare over and over.

But this time, he wasn't in the chair anymore. He could move his limbs. He was lying on his back on a mattress pushed against the wall, in the darkest part of the basement. His ankle was chained to one of the furnace's poles. The chain gave him about five feet of freedom in each direction.

The snapping sound of a lock smashed the utter silence of the basement, which had been silent but for his own labored breathing. The door opened with a long creaking sound. He found himself holding his breath. Then he heard the steps. She wore heels, judging from the neat beats on the wooden steps.

He lowered his head just a bit to glance toward the staircase. Black tights, black lacquered heels. A Scottish style skirt with green and red squares on it. From where she stood, which must have been on the fourth to last step of the stairs, he couldn't see the top half of her body. But he didn't need to. He knew exactly who she was. She stood there for a long time.

"Why are you doing this to me?" he asked finally in a

childish voice that echoed in the room.

There was no response to that question.

"Please, let me go. Do you want money? I can help you with whatever you need," he cried out hopelessly. "Why are you doing this to me?"

She stood still for a few seconds, and then she walked all the way down and towards him. Her pace was unnaturally slow. When she was close enough, he could see her again, in the room's feeble light. There was something different in her eyes. It occurred to him that even if she looked exactly like the woman he had spent the night with, she was not the same person. At all. There was something different.

Something's broken.

She walked slowly toward him.

"*She* says I cannot let you go", she whispered. "I'm sorry." There was sadness in her eyes. She kissed him on his cheek and then on his lips.

"Who? Who is she?" he cried out loud.

She leaned toward him to whisper again in his ear.

"You're free from the chair, but that doesn't mean you can leave."

The way she enunciated the word made her sound like it wasn't her decision, and it did not depend on her if he was chained down in her own basement; it was *her* decision, not hers.

"Don't try to leave," she admonished. She nodded down at her hand.

He looked down and saw a taser stick. She rubbed it gently against his naked flank. It was cold on his skin.

"*She* will make me use it on you if you don't behave."

"Who—"

"Don't let her find my diary," she said, handing him the sandwich and the journal. "I love you, Johnny."

She kissed him once more on his lips. Then, he looked her straight in the eyes.

There were infinite layers of darkness in them. Thousands beyond the darkest he could have imagined. A million times darker than the pitch-black he could see when he closed his eyes. An abyss with no bottom, with no gravity. And Wendy Jag was in the process of being swallowed by it.

"Please don't leave me here. Please, Wendy." He sobbed silently as she walked away from him.

"Don't let *her* find it," she said, without turning. She stopped at the bottom of the stairs. Her whole body shook, as if a slow, deep shiver had crossed it from head to toe. She stood there.

"Wendy?" He stretched his right arm in front of him. "Come back here, please? We can figure this out together."

"*Don't let her find it!*" she screamed in a horrendous new voice that did not belong to her. It came from the darkness. It was almost manly, as if she was trying to do the impression of a very angry man.

"Wendy?"

She didn't respond and made to go up the stairs.

"Where are you going? Don't leave me here." His voice

switched from despair to anger. "You fucking bitch. You can't leave me in here."

The woman turned back and sprang towards him. She pushed the taser stick into his abdomen. The electric current flowed through his body. It burned so badly that he thought he was going to catch on fire. But he couldn't do anything but convulse and observe the pain. Every muscle of his body was crippled. A thin layer of white drool formed at the corner of his mouth. His bladder let go. Then she stopped and went back upstairs.

He panted heavily as the air rasped in his lungs. His cheek rested on the cold slate.

Then everything went dark again.

CHAPTER NINE:

THE SWING BENEATH
THE STARS

1

July 8th, 2018

The time on his phone read 10:55 when Jamie opened his eyes. He felt thoroughly rested for the first time in a long while. He was on the soft, creaking couch placed in the middle of Mr. Bowl's living room. It wasn't a big couch; in fact, his feet dangled off the edge of it, but it was so comfortable that he had preferred it to the bed. The room was flooded with daylight, and the warm summer wind moved the curtains in the kitchen. The back door was wide open. He had spent the past couple of days reading, writing, and truly recovering from the tough days on the road. It felt like a real vacation, and the results were evident in his journal. He hadn't been this prolific in a while with his writing.

How beautiful is this picture, he thought; *how perfect is this moment?* He wished he could take an eternal, sensorial photograph of it, and use it every time he needed some peace of mind. He closed his eyes and enjoyed the gentle touch of the wind. *Should I really go to L.A.? Should I stop here?* He mused on the absurd idea for a moment. *Would Mr. Bowl let me pay rent? I could find a job and get Molly and my mother here. They would love the place. Is this wind the reason why I am thinking about it? What about this wind? What about this peace?*

The need to urinate took him back to reality. He got up and fulfilled his corporeal needs. He poured himself a cup of coffee and walked out through the back door, where he found Edward Bowl sitting silently with his cup of steaming coffee.

"Long days and pleasant nights!" the boy quoted.

Ed Bowl turned and after a few seconds said, "May you have twice the number."

"You read *The Dark Tower*?" Jamie asked, astonished.

"Now you are offending me, son. It was a long time ago, but I still have something left in this rusty box," he said, pointing at his head.

Jamie sat in silence for a while, sipping coffee and enjoying the morning air, still not spoiled by the heat. He noticed Edward's hand tremble when he brought the mug close to him.

"I like it here. It's so peaceful and quiet," Jamie said.

Edward nodded and took a sip of coffee. His features were not those of a man relaxing on the back porch, nor those of a man enjoying the beauty of the landscape in front of him.

"It is indeed a quiet place," he finally muttered in a raspy voice. "I'm not so sure about how peaceful it is."

Jamie nodded, wondering what he meant.

"This place," Edward continued. "This place is not a peaceful one. I've seen things around here that I still don't understand, when I go to sleep at night. My mother used to think that I had a spell on me. She used to say spell, but I know she meant a curse. She just tried to make it sound sweeter. My mother was a wise woman.

"You know, son, I don't know why I'm telling this to you. I guess old men like to tell stories. I don't get to speak with many people these days."

"I would love to hear one," Jamie said. "What spell?"

"She thought it was a curse. I've always known that from the way she looked at me. Sometimes she seemed scared. But she didn't want to scare me with her fears. You know, she used to pray every night, for about an hour. I could hear her murmurings from my bed; the door was always open. But when I had those episodes, she kept praying for hours."

"What episodes?" Jamie asked.

Mr. Bowl frowned. The breeze had stopped, and the air was still.

"Have you ever had the feeling that something bad was going to happen? A premonition, a bad gut feeling...I would ignore it at first but then it would happen. I quickly got to the point where the word coincidence was not a satisfying explanation anymore."

The man's eyes were lost in the space in front of him.

"It came like a dark wind on me, and it hit me hard. Sometimes it was physical contact, a handshake; sometimes it was just enough to stay close to someone to feel it. I knew when something bad was going to happen. There is no way to put this into words or try to formulate a logical explanation. I accepted the fact that some things cannot be understood, not without risking being put in a mental institute. So I kept it for myself. The unspeakable was in front of me. I could almost smell it, the rotting, putrescent cologne of malevolence. My mom saw it in me. Maybe she had it too. Perhaps I inherited it from her...

"I remember the first time very well: I was ten years old. It was Sunday, and I was dressed for church. My parents and I were in the car. I remember my dad pulling into the gas station and getting out of the car. I was in the back seat, looking out the window. There was a man refilling at the pump. I knew he wasn't from around here; I'd never seen him before. He was skinny, very skinny, with a white stained undershirt. He looked dirty. He drove a black car, I'm not sure what model it was, but it looked like a fast one to me. I was staring at him when his eyes met mine. He stood there looking at me as he refilled, and I had this terrible feeling. I could feel screams inside my head. I remember there was this low, eerie sound, like a long and lazy bellow, in the background.

"I tried to divert my eyes from him, but it was impossible. I cannot forget his eyes even to this day. Those eyes were evil. I knew something bad was going to happen that day, and that this man was going to be involved. Somehow, he would cause pain.

"When he finished refilling, he jumped back in the car, not without giving me a final glance. He didn't look angry or threatening, but something in his eyes was not right. Those eyes were filled with something that I cannot put exactly into words. He took off, and the feeling went away suddenly, as if he had taken it away with him. As if it was him."

Jamie felt like a kid being told scary stories in front of a fire. He loved it, but he couldn't tell the same about Mr. Bowl. His eyes were gloomy, as if he was going through physical pain as he evoked the events.

"What happened then?" Jamie asked.

"We headed home, but when we tried to make a left on Main Street, the road was blocked. The sheriff's car was parked across in the middle of the street, lights flashing. I can still remember the shapes of the bodies on the street, the blood—a lot of blood— and the black car, upside down. My mom looked at me and saw that I was crying. She leaned over to cover my eyes. It was a big thing in a small town like Copper City. Three kids were killed; they bled out and died on the street before the ambulance arrived. There was no trace of the man driving the black car. He had vanished, like a ghost. Nobody could ever give justice to those families."

Jamie shivered. He could see that the old man wanted to talk more; that for him, telling this story was painful and cathartic at the same time.

"I've had many others of these episodes in my life. They all happened here. This town may be quiet, agreed on that, but I don't know about the peacefulness around here. I've never been able to discern if it was just my 'gift' to make it look doomed or if it really was. I thought about moving so many times, but I never had the guts to do it. This is the only home I have, after all, the only place I know."

"Did you ever tell anyone?"

"Nobody would have believed me. And son, when the darkness touched my own family, I couldn't believe myself either."

"What do you mean?" Jamie asked.

"It's been almost thirty years..." he started after a brief pause. "My wife, Linda, she was a nurse at that time. I drove her to work every day. I made a lot of mistakes in my life, son. I had an affair with another woman at that time, and Linda knew. Not because I had the balls to tell her or because she had caught me. But deep down inside her she knew, and she never told me anything about it. I could tell from her eyes. I guess she wanted to see if I would ever tell her. I loved her, oh! I love her so much these days..." He stopped and used his neckerchief to blow his nose. Tears came down and his face was a grimace of pain from a wound that hadn't healed over and probably never would.

"One day I was driving her to work, as usual. From our house to the hospital where she worked it was a little less than a twenty-minute drive. We used to listen to this local rock 'n roll station that played many of the songs we used to dance to. On that day, she turned the radio off. It was a silent ride, a long one. I asked her what was wrong, and she said she had a headache. Something was slightly off in her smile. I think about that smile every day of my life, and the more I think about it the more I'm convinced it wasn't a smile. It was a grimace. We arrived at the hospital. Normally she would get out of the car and tell me that she loved me from the window, before turning and walking in the hospital, before disappearing behind the entrance glass doors. But not that day. That day she looked at me for the longest time, and then she kissed me. It wasn't a normal kiss. Nothing was normal on that day. I should have known better. Then she got out of the car, walked into the hospital, and did not turn back. That was the last time I saw her alive."

"What happened?" Jamie asked.

"I went back to work at the station in Albuquerque. I don't even remember what happened on that day at work. The only thing I could think of was that kiss. It was a cold one. My lips felt like freezing. When I clocked out, I stopped at a flower shop and got a few white roses for Linda. They were her favorite. I wanted to make a little gesture for her. I also decided that I would end my affair. You know, I really had a mindset change on that day, and I wanted the flowers to be the start.

"Linda used to take the bus back home after work. She always arrived home before me, but I wanted to arrive first on that day and surprise her with the flowers. Diana, my daughter, used to hang out at a girlfriend's place every day after school. I made it home at four in the afternoon, on the dot. I had a good half hour before the bus would drop her on the driveway. I parked the car two blocks after the house so she wouldn't see it. I walked.

"I opened the door and..." Edward paused for a second and looked up, as if he had the scene right in front of him. A tear came down on his face "...and she was there already. She hung herself in the entrance, from the staircase."

"I'm so sorry, Ed," Jamie said.

"You know, the autopsy said she died about twenty minutes before I got there."

"But you couldn't have known that."

"Well, that's where you are wrong, Jamie. I knew it. I knew it was going to happen. I just didn't read the signs properly."

"How?" Jamie's features tensed with curiosity and disbelief.

"It took me a little bit to go through all these events in my mind. It took years to find an answer that really made sense. Before she got out of the car that morning, she kissed me without saying a word. Her lips were gelid, Jamie. Her lips were so cold. They were cold because *something* had already taken her. They were cold as if she was already dead."

2

Edward came back from the kitchen with two steaming mugs, which suggested to Jamie that the story wasn't quite over. He had been wanting to ask Mr. Bowl if he was aware that a traumatic event could distort the memories and the perception of the event itself before it happened. He had meant to tell him that it was normal to go over and over the events, but he did not dare. On top of all that, Edward Bowl didn't appear to have any sign of dementia. Quite oppositely, he seemed to be a brilliant and wise man.

His pace was slow and trembling, so Jamie rushed toward him and got the mugs.

"So...you think I'm crazy? Don't you? You can tell me your honest thoughts. You might think that the tumor in my brain is pushing the wrong buttons. And I wouldn't blame you if you did."

"I think that's quite a story, the one you just told me. I'm sure you will allow me the benefit of the doubt," Jamie said in a calm and relaxed tone, which surprised Mr. Bowl, who nodded at him with a sympathetic smile. Jamie lit a cigarette, making sure to blow the smoke away from Mr. Bowl, looking toward the desert. How much energy there was, he thought, in the emptiness of the desert. He closed his eyes, tasting that great feeling of connection. He dreamed about finishing his novel here, in the hills.

"Have you heard from your friend today?" Edward asked.

"I haven't. I guess he's having a good time," Jamie answered with his eyes still closed. "Are you worried about him?" he asked, laughing.

"I'm an old piece of machinery, Jamie; it's in my nature to worry about things." He chuckled. "I'm actually debating with myself if it was wise of me to give him Wendy's number."

"Why's that? It was pretty clear they could not get their eyes off one another."

The old man stared straight ahead thoughtfully as his forehead crumpled in the center. "So you haven't heard from Johnny at all, have you?" he asked the boy again in a forced, flat tone that clashed with his concerned features.

"I haven't. Why should I have?" Jamie took his sunglasses off and sat straight on the chair, feeling a shudder of discomfort creeping up through his spine.

"I'm probably just overthinking," he said. He levered on his thin arms to get up, and then he stretched his back with a groan. "Are you hungry? Let's go fix some breakfast."

3

Johnny woke up on the thin mattress resting on the slate next to the dentist's chair. He had pissed his pants again after the last round with the taser stick. The sun flooded the basement, gilding the stone walls. Half awake, he could hear birds warbling outside. His left flank was burned as well as all the other areas where she used the stick on him, and he winced when his memory started to come back. Mixed voices crowded his mind.

He had completely lost track of time. He must have been down there a few days by now. She hadn't give him anything to eat. Just the daily bottle of water. He would have given everything for food.

Don't try to leave, those words echoed in the back of his mind.

That hideous voice.

He straightened himself up and looked at his burned flank. He shivered when he thought about that whirring sound and then the river of current invading him up to his lungs, biting everywhere, the heat, the buzzing in his head, and the useless effort to gasp for one more breath.

The chain was long enough to let him rest on either the chair or the mattress, to let him reach the restroom—which consisted of a bucket with a lid, placed behind the chair—and to walk around a little bit. He had probably five, six feet of reach radius at most. Of course, it had been properly measured so that he couldn't reach anything useful to him.

Don't try to leave.

He rested with his back against the wall, taking a few deep breaths. His body ached all over and his mouth tasted terrible. He was sure he hadn't ingested anything in days. He thought about that last meal he had with Wendy at the Old Junction. So much had changed in such a short time. The discomfort coming from the open wounds in his mouth was worse than ever. He had entered into an unexplored region of his mind, where the survival instinct was stronger than the pain, stronger than the terror that lived in his stomach, in his chest, and in his spine.

He downed the bottle of water that had been left for him. His nerves were frayed, and he felt a terrifying desire to laugh and cry at the same time. A raspy whine came out of his mouth. He put his fists on his temples, and more memories of Wendy came back.

Don't let her find it. I love you, Johnny.

He screamed with rage in the empty room.

Don't let her find it. Don't let her find it, Johnny.

Don't let her find what?

I love you, Johnny. Don't let her find my...

Don't let her find my...

Don't let her find my...

"Diary!" he whispered, opening his eyes. "Don't let her find my fucking diary."

He remembered now. He groped the wall behind him. He stood up slowly, bracing himself against the wall. His knees creaked loudly in the silent room, but he managed to stay on his feet. He closed his eyes, traveling through his memories once more.

She might have found it, he thought. *When I fell down, it might have dropped from my hands.*

Don't let her find my diary. I love you, Johnny.

He sat back against the cold concrete wall and cried. It occurred to him that this might very likely be the end, the last stop. How had things escalated so quickly? *How the fuck did I get into this mess?*

He was about to lose it when something caught his

attention. From his lower angle he saw the journal underneath the chair. He stretched and grabbed it, holding it to his chest like a treasure. The last time he had held this book in his hands, he'd felt guilty for breaching her privacy. This time, he felt only the hope that the little book might answer the questions that tormented him. This book might have been his only way out. Wendy wanted him to have it, to not let *her* find it.

He opened the diary and began to read about Wendy Jag's life.

October 15, 1992

Dear diary,

Mrs. Gable says that if I write here when I am sad, I will feel better. I thought all afternoon how I should name you, but then I realized it would be silly to give you a name because you are not a person. So I will just call you diary.

My name is Wendy Jag and I'm six years old. I go to Copper City Elementary School. The other kids are mean to me. They always talk bad about Daddy. But I don't listen to them. I know my daddy is the best in the whole world. My best friends are Ben, Roger, and Mr. Bowl.

Ben is my bear; he is brown and he is ten years old. He only speaks with me because I am the only one he trusts. Mr. Bowl is a very good man. He takes care of the yard and fixes everything that gets broken in the house. My daddy knows how to fix things too, but he is very busy, so Mr. Bowl helps him. He lives in a little house behind ours. We gave it to him so he could have a place to live. One day Mr. Bowl brought me a bunny. It was the cutest bunny and I asked him if I could keep it and he said I could. I named it Roger and he is a cute little naughty boy.

My mom died two months ago.

Good night, diary.

4

Jamie finished washing the last plate in the sink and put it on the draining rack with all the others. He stepped out into the back yard and stopped at the doorstep to light a Marlboro. He looked at Mr. Bowl sitting outside. He looked pale, and Jamie could clearly read the distress in his features.

"What's on your mind?" the man asked, walking toward him.

"Not much. Just enjoying the weather."

"Come on, man. I can tell you're worried about something. Is it about your omens?"

"It is indeed, son. I get you don't believe me and, to be completely honest with you, I don't blame you. The PTSD, the tumor, my age; you could really list all the medical reasons. Something bad is going to happen and I don't know how to stop it. Did you hear from your friend?"

"I did not. And, by the way, I don't judge you and what you say. I don't think what you said is bullshit. Hard to believe?

Maybe. But how many other things are so?" Jamie took a seat in front of him, took a long draw, and crossed his legs. "You have my attention. Why do you keep asking about Johnny?"

Ed sighed and diverted his gaze over the hills, pondering if it was worth going ahead or just dropping it.

"It's about Wendy," the old man finally admitted. "There is something off about her. I haven't felt this in a long time."

"What about her?" Jamie asked.

"You know, I've been working quite a long time for her father at the house. I kept the yards, landscape, and whatever plumbing or electrical work the house needed. The doc—everyone used to call him that, even though he was a dentist—was wealthy and paid well. I've never been sure of this, but I believe he overpaid me because he was lonely. He liked the company. We became friends in time.

"As we got closer, I got to do more and more fixing around the house, sometimes a shingle, sometimes the refrigerator door, and sometimes I was keeping an eye on Wendy when he had a very busy day of work.

"Theodore's wife had always been sick. She spent most of her time in her bedroom, with terrible headaches. Sometimes I could hear her screams from the back yard, even when the mower was on. The day she died, I stopped at the pet store and bought a white bunny for Wendy, to cheer her up. She named him Roger. I never considered myself part of that family, but I was close enough to live the worst and best days as a privileged external observer.

"Theo started to drink. I mean, to drink a lot. I witnessed powerlessly the pain devouring him. He began to use some drugs. Ketamine, I believe, as he had access to that for his patients. I tried to talk to him many times, but he would get mad and tell me to mind my own business.

"I could have reported that to the police. I thought about it several times."

"Why did you decide not to?" Jamie asked.

"Hard to say. It is a decision I regret to this day. I could have sent him to rehab or done something. I don't know. I was consumed by my own personal tragedy, and so was he. In a way I felt connected to him in that sense. And honestly, once I stopped being a cop, I stopped for good. I was done with that.

"I was close enough to be helpful but never gained that trust to talk about the stuff that mattered. I thought that some talk would have helped him, but I was wrong. Some people react in their own way, so all I decided to do for him, during that time, was to take care of Wendy. At that point in my life I had no family anymore. My daughter, Diana, didn't want to see me or talk to me. As a matter of fact, she still doesn't these days. She must have heard of my affair from gossip in town, so after my wife's death, she moved in with her aunt, my wife's sister. They live in Maine. So, I did really find comfort in taking care of Wendy. I know it may sound weird, but at times I pretended she was my little Diana."

A slow, relentless tear carved a path down Edward's wrinkled cheek. Jamie put a hand on the old man's knee and nodded.

"You said there was something off with Wendy." Jamal tried to control his voice as a sense of uneasiness invaded his stomach.

"At some point Theodore stopped waking up on time for his morning appointments. I would make excuses with his patients waiting for endless minutes, knocking at his door. He was there and he wasn't. At that point he had basically stopped seeing patients. He would lock himself into the basement for hours, in his world. Sometimes I could hear his screams from outside, while I was working in the back yard. I tried to confront him many times. To let him know he wasn't alone. But he made it clear that if I wanted to keep working at the house I should mind my own business.

"Wendy worshipped her father. He was her whole world, even before her mom died. And she wasn't blind. She could see that something was taking her dad away from her. She began to have troubles at school, being violent with the other kids. One day the doc had to drive to her school because she pulled a lock of a little girl's hair right out of her scalp. Theodore would later tell me that, when she was questioned by the teacher, she kept saying that the Tooth Fairy had told her to do so."

"Jesus Christ," Jamie whispered.

"But there was one day in particular that I still remember so vividly. On that day I knew something wasn't right. It was around Christmas time. I remember it was such a beautiful day, the kind when the air feels so crisp and dry that you cannot stay inside. Theodore was working in the basement, and I was on the roof, cleaning the drainpipes. Wendy was playing in the grass. She was drawing something and feeding the bunny. I could see the whole back yard from where I was, so I stopped to enjoy the scene.

"She grabbed the bunny and hugged it. At least that's what I thought at that moment. She dropped the carrot and put both her tiny hands around its neck and tightened. I tried to yell at her, but nothing came out of my mouth. Once more in my life, I saw that darkness, and I was paralyzed by it. I saw the bunny's legs and body shaking. And I cannot forget Wendy's panting, the way she gasped for air as she strangled the poor little thing. It was like she was strangling herself. She had loved that bunny so much, but something snapped in her head, in a matter of seconds. When she was sure the bunny was dead, she went around the house and put the carcass on the street, to make people think someone hit it with the car.

"When I came down to get it, I noticed that the bunny had bled out of its eyes. Initially, I thought it was because of the strangling, but after a better look, I realized that she had stabbed it in the eyes with the crayon after he was dead. She would never admit it was her. She wrapped her mind around the idea that the bunny was really hit by a car. I told her father. I told him she needed to see a doctor, to go to therapy, that something wasn't right. He would tell me that I was right and that he would call a friend of his. A pediatric psychiatrist. But then he went down to the basement to get high or drunk again. It was a very sketchy time.

"We dug a hole and buried the bunny. And she asked us how it had happened. And the scariest part was that she really didn't seem to know how it had happened."

Jamie shivered and looked at the absent light in Mr. Bowl's eyes as he collected his memories.

"Why didn't you share this with us?"

"I don't know. It was a long time ago, son. I didn't want to be unnecessarily paranoid."

His hand slipped in the front pocket of his jeans and fished out his phone. He checked the messages, the voicemail box, and the missed calls. Johnny had not called or left any message.

"Call him!" The old man's voice was louder than usual and shaken with fright.

Jamie nodded and called Johnny's number. The phone didn't even ring once. It went straight to voicemail.

5

He kept reading through the pages of the diary. Childish thoughts alternated with overly dark ones, sometimes on the same page. Johnny had quickly learned that the handwriting was somehow connected with the change of thoughts. It seemed like multiple people wrote on those pages.

He could see that one of those hands became stronger and stronger, strangling the other, the childish one, like a tumor that eats and conquers. Some things were starting to make more sense, but that didn't make him feel any better. If anything, the burden that settled on his chest became heavier, and the nausea was worse than ever. Every part of his body ached. On top of that he felt a cold tingling down his back, from his neck all the way down to the base of his spine, which he associated with the primordial instinct that was aiming to prepare him for survival.

The door slammed hard against the stonewall on top of the stairwell, and a clunking noise echoed loudly in the room. Johnny started, and the diary fell from his hands on the mattress. The steps on the wood were quick. He grabbed the diary and slipped it underneath the mattress.

The woman who stood in front of him wore a light green gown and that white wax mask with a long black wig attached to it. A baseball bat hung loosely between her fingertips. She had the taser stick in the other hand. She stood still, staring at him. The mask was of the kind people wore for carnival, with hollow dark orbs for eyes and crimson painted lips. The dark-haired wig was an addition, as the gap on the forehead suggested.

She pointed the bat toward the dental chair on his left.

"Please, please don't…" He faltered as his face crumpled, as if he could already feel the coming pain.

Her arm held the bat firmly, still pointed toward the chair. She was so still that it seemed as if she had stopped breathing. He began to crawl toward the chair, looking up at her like a dog that was just waiting to be hit.

When he was about a foot away, the bat swung and hit

him hard in the face. The pain exploded as he felt his nose smashing. He landed on his back and tried to breathe as the blood gushed copiously from his nose. The pain was so intense that he thought he was going to faint, but he did not. He wanted to scream, but only a weak whimper exhaled from his mouth. The blood ran thickly in his throat, tasting like iron. He swallowed while waiting for the intolerable pain to diminish.

She let the bat fall on the floor, and he flinched at the noise. She stooped and gently placed a bandage on his face, completely covering his mouth and nose.

It had the sweet smell of a disinfectant. It smelled like a hospital hallway would smell just after the cleaning was done. He felt the energy abandoning his limbs. His head was light.

Then the pain was gone, and it was dark again.

6

When he woke up, the first thing he could focus on was some kind of drawing. From that distance it looked like it was drawn with colored chalks. A man and a little girl stood under a starry sky, hand in hand. The letters "D&W" stuck out in white chalk at the bottom, like a signature on a famous painting.

It was hard to localize where the pain was coming from. He was in and out of a dream. He wondered if this was what death felt like. An eternal scuba dive between dream and consciousness. It wouldn't have been so bad if it wasn't for the pain, he thought. He couldn't move at all. He couldn't even tell if he still had limbs.

As his vision improved, he realized that he was supine and that the picture was chalked on the ceiling. Something was in his nostrils, and he was breathing through his mouth. He tried to close his mouth but he couldn't. Something had been placed between his jaws. The sounds around him were diminished, as if his ears were covered.

He looked down, trying to catch a glimpse of his body, and saw her. She still had the mask and the wig on, and she was rummaging on the tray next to the chair. His sense of helplessness annihilated any resistance—not that he could have resisted if he wanted to—and he closed his eyes again, childishly wishing that it would all go away and that he could go back to his boring, normal life. He had never felt such a strong desire to be back in his house, to be with his wife again. But it was too late for that, and all he could do now was to hope that the pain would be tolerable, and that death would take him fast. At the same time, deep inside himself, he found out how much he wanted to survive all this. The primitive desire of living any kind of existence, to stay anchored to this world, had never been so intense.

He felt a metallic object protruding into his mouth and heard the clinking sound of it hitting against his teeth. It was cold against his tongue. He kept his eyes closed, but he knew he was awake as he began to hyperventilate. With a shiver, he realized she was probably waiting for him to regain consciousness before doing anything to him. He let out a choked and uncontrollable sob, and he opened his eyes again.

She was on top of him, so close that he could hear her breathing behind the mask. He could see those eyes behind the dark sockets of the mask. Those eyes that had attracted him so much.

"Why...why?"

She kept staring at him. Her hand was firm on the tool that she had slipped into his mouth, ready to turn the pain on. She stood there, static, as if she was tasting every drop of his fear. He could see her enjoying it behind the mask.

He rolled his eyes back to the drawing: a little girl and her father looking at the stars. Then, the pain hit and his body jerked violently against the restraints. He felt one of his teeth shattering into little splinters that landed on his tongue. Something gripped on the tooth and pulled hard. On the first pull he felt it loosening. His jaws instinctively tried to clench, but they couldn't. With the second pull, the tooth came out violently from his gums, and the pain rose to a totally new level when he felt the root being ripped apart from him.

He screamed with all the energy he had as he felt the blood spilling in his mouth and slipping down his throat. He retched twice, then heard a whirring sound as something suctioned his saliva and blood from the corner of his mouth. The pain throbbed, radiating from his mouth all the way back to his nape. He opened his eyes, still grunting and gasping for air, and saw her examining the tooth covered in blood under a table lamp next to the chair.

Then she was back on top of him. She clutched the pliers against another tooth.

7

"Nothing at all?" Edward asked with growing concern. Three hours had passed since the last time Jamie had tried to call Johnny.

"Still the voicemail," Jamie responded. He looked once more at his messages before putting the phone back in his pocket. "Do you really think we should be worried about him? I mean, how do we know they're not just having fun?" Jamie asked, but a sense of agitation had started to sneak in.

"I need to talk to Ross Ferris," Mr. Bowl said as they walked at his pace to El Dorado. "There isn't such a thing as privacy in Copper City. If something happened, he will know it. Worst case scenario, we will drive to Wendy's house and check with our own eyes."

It was a sunny day, and the early afternoon sun was brutal on their skin. When they arrived on Main Street, the street was flooded with people. Jamie had completely forgotten that the Fourth of July's celebrations were going on until the end of the week. Jamie opened the heavy wooden door at the entrance to the El Dorado, and a breath of cool air came out, carrying the unmistakable smell of rotten wood and beer.

The place was busy, and the Say Your Prayers band members were thanking the crowd for the warm welcome from the stand. Steve Nibbs was busy pouring beers, and the waiters were working at full pace. Ed scanned the room and eventually managed to locate Ross Ferris sitting alone at the very end of the room, far from the stand.

"Follow me, son." He started carving a path through the tables.

He took the seat in front of Ross Ferris without asking for permission. Ross Ferris, aka Empty Bottle, gave him an annoyed look in return.

"I've got some questions for you," Edward said, tilting his head to Jamie. "This young man is a friend of mine. His name is Jamal Anderson. He arrived in town with the stranger in the fancy car. Do you recall that?"

Ferris nodded, but his features remained interrogative.

"Have you seen him around lately?"

Ferris shook his head, taking a full sip from his glass of water.

"Are you sure, Ross? And by the way, what the hell is going on with you? Is that water? Are you sick?"

"I'm good. Have been clean for a few days."

"Well, that's good for you, my friend," Edward commented, surprised. Then he crossed his arms on the table and stared at Empty Bottle for a time that seemed endless.

"Have you seen him arou—"

"I ain't seen no one around, alright? But I've heard folks talking."

"What did you hear?" Edward did not let him finish.

"Voices are he and the doc's daughter were seen together at The Old Junction, just out of town. I gotta admit, I kinda envy the dude. I wouldn't mind a half hour in a room with that gal," Ross said and laughed resoundingly.

"When was that?" Jamie suddenly stepped into the conversation.

"How the hell would I know that?"

"Remember a few days ago?" Edward said, "you were telling me something about her. Something you had found at the graveyard."

"Yes, you old dog. If only you listened to me instead of-"

Empty Bottle didn't even see Mr. Bowl's hand grabbing him by the neck of his discolored red tee. He pulled it down, forcing him almost with his head on the table. People at the nearby tables stiffened.

"Listen to me really carefully, you goddamn son of a bitch. You owe me one, you remember that? Spit out what you know from that rotting mouth. Do you understand what I'm saying?" Edward's voice was low but angry and threatening enough to surprise Jamie.

Ross Ferris chugged down his glass of water.

"I've seen all sorts of shit being brought to the cemetery. You know...Folks miss their loved ones and they leave all sorts of things. But I ain't seen anything as sick as what Ms. Jag leaves on her dad's stone." Ross talked out all at once, then paused for a few seconds to catch his breath. "The last thing I've found was a tooth. It was placed in the dirt. It wasn't just there. It had been *placed* there at the base of the marble. I thought it was a tiny white stone, you know? Kind of a small pebble, maybe a pearl. So I got close to see if it was anything of value. I took a good look at it, and it wasn't a stone. It was a fucking tooth. Not a fake one. It wasn't big enough to be an adult. I believe it belonged to a child. It was a milk tooth. That's all I tried to tell you last time. And that's all I know."

"Alright, alright. Are you sure you didn't hear anything else around?" Bowl asked.

"No, man, I promise. That's all I've got," Ross replied promptly, and Edward decided he believed him.

Mr. Bowl sighed with disappointment and was about to get up when a voice from his back came unexpectedly.

"Excuse me, gentlemen..."

Jamie and Mr. Bowl turned, and their eyes met a short and incredibly elegant man. A golden Rolex stood out on his wrist. He wore a white linen shirt with the sleeves raised just below the elbows and a pair of light green trousers. "The bartender told me you might know my friend John Hawk."

8

She slammed the door shut behind her, leaving the room in silence, only broken by the sound of Johnny's trembles. He stood with his bare feet on the cool slate, his back resting on the wall. He was fighting against multiple pains. There were many but they all felt like one, condensed in his head. He came to the realization that the pain would eventually go away, but what had just happened in that basement would never leave his consciousness. He was hoping he would be lucky enough to tell someone about it one day. *Perhaps I'll have to see a shrink*, he thought. *I mean, of course I'll have to see a shrink*.

He took a few steps to his left and turned the mirror to look at himself. His face was a mask of dark, clotted blood. His nose, clearly broken, was bent sideways on the right in a boomerang shape. All around it, the purple swollen area extended all the way up to his cheekbones. Two blood-soaked pieces of cotton had been placed in both his nostrils to stop the bleeding.

Well aware that the real problem was not with his nose, he opened his mouth and a gush of blood spurted out, quickly descending along the line of his chin and landing all over his tee shirt and on the floor. He rinsed his mouth with some of the water left in the cup and spat a mix of blood and saliva—mostly blood— in the small sink on the side of the chair. When he smiled again, he saw a line of dark recesses instead of his front teeth. He couldn't tell exactly how many he was missing, but, judging from how many times he had to go through the pain, he was sure that she had pulled at least six of them.

The pain intensified, almost as if the sight had brought it back. It pulsed like a lighthouse's rotating lamp, sending him in oscillating phases of darkness and light, of hope and desperation, of lucidity and madness. He abandoned himself on the mattress and lay on his left side, facing the wall in a fetal position.

What happens when she runs out of teeth to pull out? He wondered, as the pain became worse. *Is she going to kill me*? Only the pain could temporarily tarnish these questions in his mind. And madly he found relief in both as the questions shifted the focus away from the pain, even for a couple of seconds. He tried to mentally list all the things he would do if he survived this, but nothing came to him. It was impossible to focus on anything.

He grabbed the diary from underneath the mattress and he opened it to the page where he had left it. He could recognize it easily because he made a fold at the corner of the page, a habit that had cost him many reprimands from Ellen. She hated the folds on the pages, he thought, finding himself smiling lightly at that memory.

March 17, 1993
Dear diary,

I lost my first tooth today. No, it didn't hurt. I thought my teeth were prettier but when I looked at it in my hands it was quite gross. Daddy was working downstairs, and I

couldn't wait to show it to him. I'm so excited. He said that
the Tooth Fairy will come for me tonight.

 Bye diary.

Johnny turned the yellowed page, feeling the smooth paper underneath his fingertips. *The Tooth Fairy will come for me tonight*, he thought. *That is definitely as creepy as it sounds. That's not the way I would phrase it to my daughter.*

He sighed, looking down at the journal in his hands. If he knew enough about her past—he thought inevitably of Ellen who had her master's degree in psychology and psychotherapy—then maybe he could talk to her. She gave him the diary, after all. She wanted him to keep it away from *her*.

Perhaps she wanted him to help her get away from *her*.

He opened the diary again and turned the page. He recognized the childish handwriting of the page before, but something had changed. The surface of the page was irregular. Little circular areas were deeper than others. It took him a while to realize that she had cried on that page. Tears that couldn't be flattened by the weight of the other pages or by time. This page was dated almost two weeks after the last one.

March 30, 1993
Sorry. I have been busy.

 You must have wondered if I was okay. I am okay. I met her. The Tooth Fairy. She has long black hair but she doesn't talk much. Daddy told me she wears a white mask because she is too shy. He also said that I must not talk to her because she can't hear my voice and that I must do whatever she wants. We don't want to make her mad, Daddy said.

So when she appeared at night, it was kinda scary. But my daddy told me that she would show up like that. I was expecting her. She stood still, staring at me for a while. I could feel her breathing under the mask. She must have been hot. She sat on the bed and touched my leg. I wanted to say something but Daddy said not to talk to her. She stood up and looked like she wanted me to follow her. So I followed her.

She wanted to go down in the basement. Daddy knew everything. He told me she was playful and that all she wanted was to play with me. After that she would take the tooth under my pillow and the morning after I would find a surprise. She made me lie on the chair where Daddy cures his patients. I was going to tell her that Daddy does not want me to play around where he works, but she put a finger on her mouth, so I was reminded not to talk. She took her clothes off and wanted me to do the same.

It was cold so after I did she gave me a blanket. I was on the chair and she opened my legs.

She told me to close my eyes. I have never played that game before. She kissed me and I could feel the same smell that Daddy has when he drinks and cries for my mom.

*I tried to remember but I can't. There were a lot of stars.
I was on a swing. And Daddy pushed me.*

*If you only could see. There were so many stars in the
sky.*

9

The old Chevy truck revved loudly, going up on the hills,
well above the speed limit, on the jolty dirt road that twisted
through Copper City. The dry and still warm air of midsummer
elbowed its way into the vehicle from the opened windows.

Jamie sat in the back seat, his arm out of the window,
moving his hand to split the air. He thought about Johnny. He
wondered if he was in real danger or if Mr. Bowl was really
losing it. What if he just left? He didn't have any obligation to
tell him. *The man gave me a long ride until here. He gave me
money, food, a place to sleep, made me feel like a fucking human
being again*, he thought. *How isn't that enough to you, Jamie?* he
wondered, letting the bitter sense of loss dissolve in the back
of his mind. *Are we even friends?* Jamie thought. But the truth
was that it didn't seem to be like him to just leave in such a way.
His stuff was still at Mr. Bowl's place. This option didn't make
any sense at all. The concern grew on his features as well with a
sense of discomfort that took place in his stomach.

Edward Bowl pushed the gas pedal as the road got steeper.

Gregory Bollard sat in the passenger seat, looking out of the window and shaking his head. Mr. Bowl had told him all they knew about Johnny's disappearance, along with giving a clear summary of Wendy Jag's background.

"He must be some sort of magnet..." Greg said in a dried-out voice.

"Uh? What did you say?" Edward had to yell to be heard in the old truck.

"I don't know how Johnny does it, but he has this ability, you know, to attract people that are not good for him." There was a tremble of serious concern in his voice, Edward reckoned.

"We will find him," Edward told him and nodded as if he was trying to convince himself.

"Should we call the police, Mr. Bowl?" Jamie joined the conversation from the back seat.

"Not if we can avoid it," he responded promptly, looking at Jamie through the rearview mirror. "I'm honestly not even sure that she has anything to do with it."

"Why don't we go straight to her place, then?" Jamie insisted.

"I need to check something first. We're almost there."

The truck reached the top of the hill. The air was cooler there. *This must be one of the tallest places around here*, Jamie thought, looking down at the valley. The street ended into an open space. Edward took the car to a halt in front of an iron gate. Mr. Bowl stopped the car and they all jumped out. Only then did they understand where they were.

The graves stood silently in tidy rows, following the slope of the side of the hill that faced north. The silence was so utter that even the wind didn't dare to disturb it.

Edward gestured for them to follow him as he unbound the chain on the other side of the gate. It opened, welcoming them with a prolonged squealing sound.

Jamie looked at the short rows of tombstones. Some of them seemed very recent, judging from the modern layout of the letters engraved in them. Some others were so old that he could hardly read the names and the years on them. One of them didn't even have a stone, just a bunch of dead flowers resting on the soil. Weeds had grown all over.

The graves followed the hill's curvature on the north side. Despite the faltering pace, Edward seemed to be in a hurry. Jamie gazed to his left, toward Greg. He looked sincerely worried. He kept checking his phone. Their eyes met for a moment, and Jamie showed him his most empathic face. "Don't worry. We'll find him. I'm sure he's okay. He must be having the time of his life with that girl," Jamie said.

Greg shrugged, returning a weak smile. "What the hell are we doing in a graveyard?"

"I have no idea," Jamie whispered to him as they followed Edward.

He knelt before a large, rectangular stone. Compared to the others, it was extremely tidy. Two bunches of fresh flowers rested in two tall glass vases on either side of the stone. The grass around the dark grey stone was the only mowed area of the cemetery.

Jamie turned around to read the name on the granite, and a shiver crossed his spine:

Theodor William Jag
"Doc"
1955 - 1995

Jamie followed Mr. Bowl's hand as he reached a childish drawing taped to the stone. He unfolded it and looked at it for a long time, as if he was expecting it to tell him something useful. It was the typical drawing a kid would do about their family: a mom, dad, child, and a creepy figure on the right, holding the kid's hand. Ed held the piece of paper in his hands and closed his eyes, trying to focus. A couple of minutes passed before he put it back where it was, yelling his frustration out.

"It doesn't work," he said, looking at Jamie. "It should work."

Only then did Jamie understand what Mr. Bowl was trying to do. He was looking for his omen to appear. He had mentioned that sometimes touching things could give him that feeling of darkness.

The echo of thunder roared in the distance.

"Do you have the number of this girl, Wendy?" Greg decided to step in.

"I do," Edward uttered, pulling himself up. "I just wanted to try this first."

"Try what, exactly?" he replied with a mixed tone of

impatience and wonder at the same time. "You said he was seen with her a couple of nights ago. What are we waiting for?"

Mr. Bowl nodded and fished his phone out of his pocket. "Let me talk to her," he said. "I'll put her on speaker."

CHAPTER TEN:

A STORM IS COMING

1

The phone vibrated loudly on the white marble kitchen counter. *She* looked at it and let it ring for a few seconds. *She* had been waiting for this moment. It was inevitable, but *she* was prepared.

She had shut the blinds in the house, as she would normally do when she left to go back to Albuquerque, to her vile, nauseating, fake normal life. But not this time. If this worked out as *she* had planned, it would buy her enough time to clean everything up. She had repeated in her mind countless times the list of actions that would guarantee her invisibility. No traces of any kind were left. No judge would sign a warrant based on the mere fact that she had been seen at dinner with Johnny Hawk. If she played her cards well, she could have a little more fun before she dissolved him into nothing.

The feeling of power and total control turned her on, and she bit her lower lip hard to kick those thoughts to the back of her mind. It wasn't the right time.

After the fifth ring, she cleared her voice out and picked up the call.

"Hello," she said, faking a slightly sleepy voice.

"*Wendy? Wendy, dear. It's Edward.*" The old man's voice sounded crackly. "*Am I disturbing you?*"

"No, not at all. Are you alright?"

"*Yes...yes, I'm good. Hey, listen, is Johnny there with you?*"

The old man wanted to play detective. He had been one after all, in another life. Just as she had forecasted. He hadn't gone to the police.

She paused for a second. She knew she needed to pace herself in the conversation to be credible. She wanted to build a sense of uneasiness with the question he had just raised.

"Uhm. Please don't judge me, Edward. It's quite embarrassing and I already feel pretty lousy." Another long pause followed by a deep sigh, which she wanted to make sure he heard loud and clear. "I didn't know he was married."

The silence on the other side of the phone was music to her ears. She could almost see the old man blushing, feeling ashamed for even having asked where he was.

"*I'm not here to judge you, Wendy. I don't have, by any means, the intention to get into your private life, but Johnny—his friends here, they're concerned. They haven't heard anything from him in a few days. Is he there with you?*"

"No, he's not. We went out for a date on Tuesday. He left the day after in the morning. You know what men do, right?

They seduce you; they get what they want from you, and then they leave. Without even having the courage to say bye to your face. He thought that I didn't deserve that. He just left me with a text. I guess that was enough for him to be at peace with his conscience."

She got ready for the best part. She had played this conversation in her mind over and over, perfecting every detail, like an actor obsessed with the right tones and pace. So she hoped that self-preparation would serve its purpose. She couldn't get this part wrong. She sobbed lightly twice, being very careful not to overdo it. She needed to show she was hurt, but she couldn't sound like a sixteen-year-old that pulled down her panties too easily.

She heard other people's voices in the background. He must have put her on speaker. There were a few seconds of silence before Edward Bowl resumed the conversation.

"*Do you have any clue where he could be?*"

She felt almost disappointed that they were already at this point in the conversation. She took her time savoring their blindness and stupidity. She had used his fingerprints to access his phone and go through all his messages—of course, only after disabling the GPS and putting the phone in Airplane Mode so it couldn't be tracked. One could learn a lot from all the data stored in a phone these days. It was like being given free access to Johnny Hawk's life for the past year.

She knew exactly what direction she had to point them, but she had to do it in the right way. Too much information would sound suspicious. She picked the right pieces of the puzzle and put them in order, in front of their nose, like a trail of treats for dogs.

"When we were at dinner, he mentioned he was going to visit his best friend in L.A. I think the guy's name was Greg."

There was a moment of utter silence on the other side of the phone. That morning, she had read that Greg Bollard had come to town because Johnny wasn't returning his messages. She had been perspicacious enough to go through all of his messages in the past months. A lot of them were from his wife, Ellen. He had stopped returning her messages after one day in May. He barely responded to Greg Bollard, too—just a few short texts to let him know he was alive. Johnny Hawk was clearly running away from the world and didn't want to be found. So that card was powerful and not too risky to play. The more she thought about it, the more she loved the way it slotted in the pieces of the puzzle she had carefully built.

She felt her muscles relaxing, her breathing getting back in total control, her heartbeat almost too slow. They must feel like a bunch of idiots, she thought, getting worried for their friend and considering the thought that maybe they had overthought that, feeling even guilty for having doubted a woman who had just been seduced and abandoned by the same guy.

She heard some other voice murmuring something that sounded like "*What the fuck?*"

"Are you still there, Edward?"

"*Yeah...yes,*" Mr. Bowl floundered. "*We will keep trying to*

225

contact him. Thank you, darling. You've been really helpful. Are you okay?"

"I guess so. Yeah, I'm okay. I'm back in Albuquerque. I didn't feel like staying this weekend."

"Well, bye now, sweetheart. Take care."

"You too, Ed."

2

The door clattered loudly against the unfinished brick wall, and the noise filled the basement. A rectangle of light was projected on the floor in front of Johnny Hawk. He was finding that hunger was able to bend all other thoughts and needs of the soul. His hunger had overcome the point of being a pure psychological need and reached a new dimension of disturbance. His body cramped at the simple thought of anything his mind could torture him with. He had read somewhere that the human body can survive about three weeks without food. Under normal circumstances, fear tended to deprive him of appetite, but these weren't normal circumstances anymore, and not even the pain could lessen his hope that food was coming.

When he realized she wasn't bringing him any food, he sank his head into his knees and rocked himself to calm down. He looked at her with tears in his eyes in an utterly submissive imploration.

She smiled, pleased, then she slowly walked backwards

without turning her back to him, placing a chair in the middle of the room and turning on the lamp that rested on the desk. Then she sat.

He looked at her without moving with fearful eyes, wondering what would come next. What were her intentions this time? What if she came down to finish him? Perhaps his end had come.

She looked at him, amused, and crossed her legs, showing a pair of dark stockings, which ended in a wider black band, perfectly contrasting with the pallor of her skin, just above her knee. He glimpsed lust in her eyes. For a moment he wanted to go back to a few days before, when they had first met. She looked exactly like the same beautiful woman, only she wasn't. Something in her mind had gone irreversibly off. He didn't have any doubt now. There were two women inside her.

He remembered a time when Ellen had talked to him about a patient with DID—dissociative identity disorder. He wondered if Wendy was aware of her other half, if they were aware of one other. And which one of the two was she now? *Why does she look so horny?*

She stood up, letting her white gown drop on the floor. She was naked, with the exception of her stockings, which were anchored to an almost invisible thong. She clumsily pirouetted so he could see her whole body. Then she giggled.

"Go to the chair," she ordered in a feeble voice.

He stayed on the mattress where he had just consumed his dinner.

"Move!" she said abruptly. "Walk to the chair."

He winced at her change in tone and then he was on his feet, his free will gone. He followed the instructions. After sitting in the chair, he turned and saw that she had taken a couple of steps forward. Her perfectly sized breasts rested at the peak of their perfection. Her nipples were hard. She looked still amused, enjoying every second of his confusion and her dominance. She could have ended him right now, just using the taser stick that he knew she was hiding in her right hand. Considering how damaged he was already, he thought that would be enough to kill him.

She giggled. She bit her lower lip, playing with the stick in her hand with her fingertips.

"Take your clothes off," she said, very lightly. She giggled again, like a little girl who had just said something naughty.

Johnny took his jeans off, though he couldn't completely get rid of them because of the chain on his ankle.

"The underwear as well," she ordered.

As he did, a terrible thought slipped through his mind. She was the little girl on the swing beneath the stars. He looked at the ceiling and, in one moment, everything was horribly clear in his mind. There weren't just two of them. The hell only knew how many were living inside her. She was playing with him.

His mind flashed through the pages he read in her diary.

She made me lie on the chair where Daddy cures his patients.... She took her clothes off and wanted me to do the same. I was on the chair and she opened my legs.

It was her revival, her revenge over the monster. He looked back at the ceiling as she started to walk toward him.

If you only could see. There were so many stars in the sky...

She was about three feet from him when she showed him the taser.

"This guy here, my dear, is going to hurt you a lot if you don't behave. Am I clear?" She winked at him.

Johnny shivered and the tremors restarted. The thought of the pain and the whirring sound were bad. He dropped on his knees with his hands clasped together to beg her.

"So, you are going to do exactly as I say. You will not talk. Now, stand up and come closer."

He stood up and took one step closer to her. She gently touched his face, then his shoulders and chest. Her hand went down and massaged him, caressing him as he started to get hard. He was crying in silence. Tears came down silently on his meager cheeks, steering through the untamed beard. She licked his tears, and she started moaning.

"Sit!" she said, pointing at the chair.

After he did, she reclined the back of the chair and adjusted the footrest, then pulled her thong down and climbed over him. He was about to say something, but she brought her finger to her lips and hushed him. Then she rubbed herself against him. Before she let him slip inside she showed him the switch, silently reminding him how quickly she could push it on his skin if she needed.

Then she pushed his head back on the headrest, forcing him

to look at the ceiling as she rode him. The only thing that kept him alive and active was the fear of that stick being used on him, even accidentally. The whirring sound was still loud in his mind, sending shivers all over his quivering body.

When she reached her orgasm, she screamed and strengthened her grip on his neck. She sat there until her breathing went back to normal, then stood back up and got some distance from him, still lying on the chair and afraid to even look at her from the corner of his eyes. He kept watching the ceiling.

It was about torture time again, and the thought of it re-nourished her pleasure, which never stopped flowing inside her. She looked at the stick and thought about using it. A couple of seconds too late and she could have killed him. She could have. Only she could have. She was empowered to decide when his life was over. She was torn between the decision to end him right now—because she could—or to resist that temptation and have another round at it. It took such will power, she thought, as the last piece of cake could be served twice, but one wants it all.

She pushed the stick against his chest, and it made a whirring, crackling sound as the electricity burned his hair. His eyes widened, as if another dimension of pain had been discovered. She got goosebumps and touched herself, trying to keep every single moment memorized in her mind like pictures. She watched the thin layer of white drool forming between his clamped lips and smelled the caustic scent of his skin burning.

She thought about going all the way until he was roasted, until she reached her pleasure again. *Fuck it! I want the cake and I want it all now!*

But then she stopped, and Johnny's body changed from storm to the uttermost stillness. She got close to him, just enough to check if he was breathing at all. It would be such a fucking bummer, she thought, if she couldn't use him again. She captured a small movement of his chest expanding and was glad. His breathing sounded labored and even though unconscious, he gasped for air.

Well, that was close, she thought as she walked back upstairs.

3

They were silent for the whole trip back to Bowl's place, each of them for different reasons. Edward looked into the rearview mirror and met Jamie's eyes for a tiny fraction of a second. If Edward and Greg were mainly feeling stupid, Jamie was feeling deeply betrayed. He was mad, even though he tried to mask that with indifference. The truth was that Jamie felt abandoned like a dog in a shelter. And knowing that he didn't have any right to feel like that didn't really help. Since the moment he'd been offered the ride, he had feared this moment. It didn't matter how much crap life had asked him to swallow; the hope that he had felt riding with Johnny towards L.A. was stronger than the cynicism he had been forced to learn. *We were going together, for Christ's sake*, Jamie thought. *How did he just give up on that*?

These questions crowded his mind as he got out of the truck in the gravel driveway of Mr. Bowl's house. He dragged himself heavily upstairs to take a shower. When he got into the bedroom, he looked at the bed where Johnny had slept. As Jamie ran the hot water and took his dusty clothes off, he couldn't remember one time when Johnny had been unkind to him. And remembering all that kindness made him even angrier as the water hit his skin. He took his time, letting the warm jet fall on his nape as heat relaxed his muscles, pushing away the beginning of a headache.

When he finished, as he dried himself off, his eyes fell on the gym bag resting on the floor, half-opened on the right side of the air mattress. He thought to look inside, but he felt that Greg would have been a more appropriate person to do so. So Jamie got dressed in the only clean clothes left in his backpack and took Johnny's bag downstairs. Predictably, Ed had turned a fire on in the rusty fire pit. The air was filled with the smoky smell of fire camp. Greg Bollard sat by the fire, staring into it with his phone still in his hands, ready to pick up if Johnny called.

Jamie threw the bag at his feet, and Greg startled.

"Why did he leave his stuff here if he was planning to take off?" Jamie asked. He pushed a Marlboro against one of the embers to light it up. "Why do such a thing? Am I the only one smelling that something is just not right here?"

"What are you trying to say?" Edward asked from behind.

They both looked at Greg, who rummaged in the bag. He

fished out a white envelope and a pocket-sized notebook. Then he turned the bag upside down in the warm light of the fire. The contents fell on the grass with a thumping sound. The men looked at one other, puzzled. In the midst of rumpled shirts and balled-up tees, Johnny's revolver glared in the tenuous light.

"I'm trying to say that something is terribly wrong here," Jamie continued. He grabbed the heavy gun in his hands, opening the cylinder and ascertaining that the gun wasn't loaded. He looked to the others, trying to find a spark of skepticism in their eyes. "This whole thing doesn't make any sense. Why would he just vanish like this? I don't pretend to know the guy as well as you, Greg, but for Christ's sake, am I really the only one thinking this is so fucking weird? He could have had all the time to come back here, get his shit, his gun. There was all the time to say goodbye. If he felt like going alone, it would have been fine by me. Why can't you see what I mean, guys?"

"What are you suggesting, son?" Edward asked again calmly, almost in a fatherly tone. "I see where you are trying to go, but..."

"There is something going on here. My friend..." He paused and looked at Greg, searching for an ally. "Our friend could be in danger."

Jamie paused and lit up another cigarette.

"What is he running away from?" Jamie asked, his eyes pointed at Greg and filled with somber curiosity. The fireworks in town had started, but they all ignored them.

Greg took a moment, trying to collect his thoughts, like a man who doesn't quite know where to start the story. Then the memories and the episodes started to flow like a river filled with nostalgia, grins and sympathetic smiles, so they could learn the story of Johnny Hawk.

4

July 9th, 2018

The next morning, Jamie woke and immediately looked at his phone on the nightstand. 7:43 a.m. No calls, no messages. Downstairs, Greg's voice echoed between the walls.

When he got downstairs, Edward and Greg were in the kitchen, talking animatedly. Mr. Bowl was on one side of the counter fixing coffee and Greg on the other, visibly jaunty.

"What's going on?" he asked from the staircase.

Jamie's eyes waited for answers with impatience.

"I got a text message from Johnny this morning. 6:30 a.m.," Greg finally said.

"What?" Jamie asked.

"Come here," Greg said, handing the phone to him.

Jamie looked at Mr. Bowl. Even though Jamie didn't know him very well, he would bet a good amount of money that it wasn't one of his good days. He looked pale and not completely able to mask his concern.

Jamie grabbed the phone, completely awake now. He saw the messages sent by Greg, on the right side of the screen: "Where are you?" and "Hello???" and "What the fuck, Johnny, call me back." The oldest ones were blue, which meant that they had been sent in a moment where Johnny's phone was active and connected to some sort of network. The last two clouds, containing the most recent messages, were green, which meant his phone was either off or that he had lost signal.

On the left side instead was one new message. Jamie read it twice.

Sorry, service is crap around here. I'm heading west.
Crossed Arizona's border a couple of hours ago and taking a
leak now at a Phillips 66. I will call you when I'm in L.A. in a
week or so. I'm okay.
It's beautiful around here.

Jamie returned the phone to Greg. He felt an uncomfortable cold shiver creeping its way along his spine. Johnny hadn't mentioned him in the text. Not a word. Not a fucking one at all. If the message was really sent by Johnny, he was clearly out of danger, and that was good. On the other hand, the text didn't seem authentic to his eyes. That was not the same Johnny he had shared a piece of road with. Jamie faked a smile and poured himself a cup of coffee. He looked at Edward massaging his temples as if the trotting migraine that was afflicting him would magically go away.

"I'm going back to L.A. today. It sounds like he's on his way, and there's no reason for me to keep bothering you two any longer," Greg said almost solemnly. "I can't thank you enough for your hospitality, Mr. Bowl."

"My pleasure. I don't get many visitors these days. It was nice to see my house full again," Edward responded in a flat tone.

"Jamie," Greg continued, turning to the young man, "I'd be more than happy to pay for your flight to L.A. From what I learned, I'm sure Johnny would be angry at me if I didn't offer you a way to get where you're going."

Jamie sipped his coffee, still too hot to be fully enjoyed. A million thoughts traveled in his mind, some of them completely unrelated to the moment. He felt the weight of the decision he had to make.

"That is really kind of you, Greg, and I thank you for the offer," Jamie started. He paused. He had a free pass to L.A., the only destination he'd had in mind since he had left his sister. He could still get there way earlier than he had originally planned. Luck was smiling at him again. He could finish his novel, find an honest job, and look for an agent, for someone willing to bet on his story. Maybe Johnny and Greg could find him a good contact.

"But I'm going to take my chances here." Jamie looked at Mr.

Bowl, who nodded back with a weak smile. "I will find a job here and I will find a place in town. Hopefully I will save some money and make it to L.A. on my own. Plus, I really don't mind it around here."

Mr. Bowl's features relaxed and he smiled, as if he had feared Jamie would leave too.

"I don't see issues with your plan, son. As I just mentioned, I really don't mind some company. And I know someone that could use some help in town during the off-seasons," Mr. Bowl replied. His eyes were greener than ever in the bright light of the morning. Jamie found them empty, distracted. Something was on his mind.

Jamie nodded to him with gratitude, then turned to Greg, who shrugged. "Alright, then. I wish you the best of luck. Here's my number," he said, handing Jamie a fancy business card. "Give me a call when you make it over to L.A."

"Thank you."

"Well, would anyone give me a ride to my rental car in town? I would use Uber, but around here I'm afraid someone's going to show up with a horse."

They all laughed and for a moment, they all felt the burden on top of their chests getting lighter.

"I was headed to town anyway. Give me about ten minutes and I'll get you there," Edward promptly offered.

5

Edward Bowl shut the door behind him and rested his back against it. *Jamie is right*, he thought. *We were right from the beginning.* He kept repeating that to himself as if he had to persuade his mind once more. A feeling of deep darkness hovered around his visual range, radiating from his temples. His head throbbed, and somehow he knew it wasn't the tumor. It was *that* feeling again, the one he had felt before. The omen. He hadn't felt it this clearly in a long time.

He rushed to the old desk on the far corner of what he liked to consider his office. The room was occupied, for the most part, by a washer and dryer, but the fact he placed a tiny wooden desk, once belonging to Diana, and that he filled it with the most important documents was enough for him to consider it his office. He opened a drawer and fished out a black notebook. He went straight to the page he needed, then picked up the phone receiver and pushed a combination of numbers on the outdated keypad.

The phone rang twice before a high-pitched feminine voice welcomed him on the other side.

"Urgent Dental Office, this is Darlene, how can I help you?"

"Good morning," Edward started, keeping his voice clear but quiet enough not to be heard from downstairs. "Could I speak with Dr. Jag, please?"

"Just one moment, sir. What is your name?"

"Rudolph—Chris Rudolph."

"One moment, please," the voice on the other side said just before an awfully irritating piece of recorded music started to hammer into the phone receiver, remarkably amplifying his discomfort.

Come on, Wendy, he thought. *Pick up the phone and show me how wrong I am; how paranoid this old piece of junk has become.* The music went on for almost a minute.

"Thank you for your patience, sir." The voice on the other side was back. "Dr. Jag is not in the office at the moment. Would you like to leave a message for her?"

"Wait; what do you mean, at the moment? If she is not available right now, I can wait until she is. Will she be in the office at some point today?"

"She called in sick, sir. Is this an emergency? If there's something I can help you with, I can direct you to another—"

Edward slammed the landline receiver down on the floor. The battery cover and the batteries flew in the air, landed on the carpet, and rolled until they finally stopped against the wall.

"Goddamn!" Edward whispered. He turned to the wall behind the desk and looked at the painting hanging there. It was a replica of an old painting, Saturn Devouring His Son by Goya. Edward paused to look at the wide-open eyes of Saturn, full of unspeakable hunger and horror at the same time, at the bloody mouth diving into the flesh.

He took the painting off the wall. Behind the painting was a small rectangular safe, engraved into the plaster wall.

He turned the knob until the lock clicked, and he pushed the handle down. Inside the safe was a copy of his will, carefully stored in a white envelope. "To Diana" was written on the front side. He put it in the central drawer of the desk, thinking how long it might rest there before Diana would open it. The thought of her being back in this house, even when he was gone, thawed his heart a little.

Then he grabbed something wrapped in a yellow microfiber rag. He gently rested it on the desk and unfolded it. When he did, the long and shiny barrel of his .44 gleamed in the light of the morning. He opened the magazine and checked if all six bullets were in there. Not without a cold shiver crossing his spine, his mind traveled to those times—at least four that he could recollect— when he had felt the cold barrel in his mouth, feeling the gentle pressure of his fingers on the trigger, considering that one little extra movement of his hand could have put an end to his life. He relived those moments every time he held the gun, getting ready for the deafening sound and the ultimate darkness.

He closed the safe and walked to the closet on the other side of the room. He opened the door and grabbed a brown leather keychain. On the back, a white label had been taped, which had smeared the ink, fresh at the time the label was written, to distinguish these keys from all the others. Edward Bowl sighed and looked out the window. Dark clouds loomed far in the distance, and purple lightning scattered in the midst of them. He wore his raincoat, placing the gun in the chest pocket on the left side, then peered back at the keychain in his hand. For a moment, he went back many years, to a time when everything was still in place.

On the label, the capital letters were still recognizable in spite of the years.

JAG PROPERTY

Just then, the door slammed open. Jamie was on the other side. Edward Bowl didn't even try, knowing Jamie wouldn't have taken no as an answer. He looked at the young man and envied his vigorous youth, his energy. Nobody could have stopped him.

"Bring a jacket," Mr. Bowl said as he finished collecting his stuff. "A storm is coming."

CHAPTER ELEVEN:

REMEMBER THAT DAY?

1

Tac...Tac...Thump!

That sequence of regular sounds seemed to come from remote distances. Johnny's eyes were closed, and he didn't have any intention of changing that. No reason to stop observing the endless flow of his thoughts. This was actually one of the most incredible moments of his entire life. There wasn't anything pleasant outside of his mind; only pain, the kind that was triggered by the light. Outside was thunder, coming stronger as minutes went by. It was so comfortable there.

Tac...Tac...Thump!

Outside, there was the hoarse groan of the air coming out of his lungs, burned in the electric shock. Outside, every breath hurt like it was the last one. Out there, his legs were numb and his head felt light. Outside, everything that could have gone wrong did go wrong. It was so dark out there.

So why should he open his eyes? Why? Everything felt so much better inside. Yes, she was coming, but opening his eyes wouldn't stop that. She was coming for him, and this time would likely be the last one. But he was safe inside. Nobody could hurt him where he was now. It was a delirium of feelings, warm touches, thoughts, and music of the best kind. Inside.

Inside, a waterfall of knowledge kept flowing thunderously and everything finally made a lot of sense. The words of the songs he kept hearing in his mind were mixed together but still perfectly recognizable. They helped him weave the thread that prevented him from getting lost in the dreadful labyrinth of darkness waiting for him outside. *But that's outside, Johnny*, he thought deeply. *It is outside. Oh no! It's so dark outside that I think I'm going blind.*

Tac...Tac...Thump!

Someone's out there, he thought. Someone wanted to break the imaginary door of his unconscious shelter, he thought, as he heard the thumping sound of angry fists on the shaky wood of his consciousness. But he was still inside, and the rest was outside.

For now.

The sudden roaring sound of thunder made him flinch, and the music went one level down, becoming less clear. He could now hear the pounding rain that stormed outside more loudly than the sound of weeping guitars, starting to fade away.

Tac... Tac... Thump!

He shivered and brought his arms around himself to feel the warm touch a little longer, finding instead the cold of his sweaty skin scattered with goosebumps. And the music was barely audible anymore. It reached his ears only with the asynchronous distorted sound of the guitars, now playing a death anthem.

It is so dark out there.

The knocking grew louder on the door now, and he brought his hands to cover his ears. Among the shattered fragments of his thoughts, one emerged stronger, and it was regretful. He regretted he hadn't found that happy place before, when he could still have enjoyed it. *Better late than never, right? Isn't that what they said?*

Tac... Tac... Thump!

He smiled and a tear fell to meet his dry lips. It was bitter. Could he have ever imagined that his mind was this singular, this colorful and magic? The thumping was so strong now that he felt it coming from inside his chest, and he realized the hinges were about to give. Just one hit away.

He wished he had listened to more music. He wished he had more time. *Don't we all, Johnny?*

But everything dies, Johnny: the flesh, the stones, our dreams, the stars themselves.

He opened his eyes and saw them, those legs. He saw the heels landing one after another on the last step.

Tac... Tac...

And he saw the butt of the rifle and her fingers—which looked now disproportionately long—wrapped around the barrel. The rifle landed heavily on her right.

Thump!

And finally the thought came, with the deafening echo of the thunder outside. It came like a wind, wiping out all the music and the sounds, inside and outside. It started as a tickle in his lungs and grew into a whisper. It crept up to his brain as an echo and mutated into a haunting scream. And the scream was dull in the silence of the room, full of acceptance.

Johnny Hawk was ready to die.

2

When she had woken up that morning, the bright sun and the gentle touch of the breeze in her dream had been replaced by pale greyness and still air. She had heard the sound of the waves breaking on the shore becoming the sound of thunder approaching. The view of the hazel wavy hair of her mom dancing in that light white dress had vanished. The feeling of thin sand slipping through her fingers was a distant memory, though still so real and fresh on her skin.

It's me, she thought—but that wasn't completely true. Not a hundred percent true. The beast was still there somewhere, resting but ready to wake up hungrier than ever, willing to swallow all that was left of Wendy.

She deeply wished to go back to her dream, to hear her mother's voice once more.

Tears came into the eyes she so strongly tried to keep shut. She just wanted to see her mom turning toward her once more. She wanted to be looked at once more with those eyes full of love, with that smile that would have melted everything. That would have sent the darkness away in a heartbeat.

But she didn't turn. Wendy couldn't see her face.

If she tried hard enough, she could still hear the notes of her mom's favorite song coming out of the old stereo that she had brought to the beach on that day. Her mom wasn't singing in the dream, though.

Look at me, Mom, she begged, *just once more. That's all I need. I won't fail you. Once more will be enough. I don't want to be taken, Mom. I just want to be with you.*

Then the beast awoke.

"*It is time...*"

"No, no, no...please."

"*...to end it.*"

The beast wasn't talking. She never did. But the eerie voice was loud in her head.

She closed her eyes and saw her mom, still facing the ocean.

"Mom, please. Look at me."

But she didn't turn. And the bright sunlight dimmed until she could barely see the white contours of her dress dancing in the wind. Then the darkness swallowed it and she opened her eyes.

The monstrous grin resurfaced on her features. Her cheeks, still wet, were unnaturally stretched. She got up and walked to the window. She peeked through the blinds at the front yard. All clear.

A front of dark clouds was quickly moving toward her. And the beast giggled in a childishly evil voice. She was pleased with that sight. She got energy from the darkness and the storm, from the clouds it carried.

3

After giving Greg a ride to his rental car, Ed and Jamie drove back out of town. They didn't talk in the car; they didn't tell Greg anything about the new suspicions that had emerged. They left the car about half a mile away from the Jags' property, down the road between two bushes big enough to cover its length. The thunder was getting closer. The air was hot and filled with dense electricity.

They cut through the bushes, following a trail that Edward knew well. He used to hike it when the work at the property ran low and also when he wanted to get away from it, to drink his pain down to the bottom of the flask.

"We'll get there from the back, and we'll check the garage first. She must have parked her car inside."

Jamie nodded nervously. Mr. Bowl looked like crap. He was as wan as a ghost, and his forehead was sweaty. The hair stuck out from the side of his head, and his breathing sounded labored and unsteady. If they weren't about to break into a private property, Jamie would think he was going to have a heart attack.

"Why don't we call the police and let them deal with it?" Jamie asked as they made their way through the first line of trees.

"They won't get in without a warrant."

"And we can?"

"Are you really asking me this, son?"

"Fair enough."

Mr. Bowl stopped when they reached a row of cypresses. The trees stood tall in broad formation, like the entrance of a dense forest. Only the locals knew that the trees surrounded the Jags' family property. Edward Bowl had worked behind these natural walls for almost half of his life. As he tried to catch his breath, a shiver crossed his back. That sensation again, grimmer than ever, reminding him that time was running out. He jerked his chin for Jamie to follow him.

"Here, this way," he said, moving to the left of the tree line. "See if you can get through. There's a hole in the fence somewhere around here. I never fixed it in twenty years, and may I be goddamned if anyone ever did."

Jamie crawled in. The thorny needles brushed his skin as the rain started to pour down. A crackly thunder roared just above his head, and he flinched, rushing toward the fence. It occurred to him to think that the last way he wanted to die was electrocuted under a tree in a god-forgotten town in New Mexico.

He snuck into the gap between the tall iron-wired fence and the trees, looking for the hole. He found it exactly where Mr. Bowl had predicted, a few feet on his left. He whistled, signaling Mr. Bowl to the exact spot, then waited, holding the net when it was Mr. Bowl's time to go through.

When they were both in, Mr. Bowl pointed to a squat building on the right, with dark green siding.

"Go around the garage and look for her car. She drives a white SUV. I'll go around the house on the other side and check the front."

Jamie nodded and started to hunch over when Mr. Bowl grabbed his arm.

"Hold on a second," he said as he reached for his pocket. He fished out a 9mm Glock and flicked the safety switch. "Red dot means safety on, no red dot is armed. You've got fifteen rounds in the magazine. Do you understand what I just said?"

Jamie swallowed and nodded, then said, "I hope I won't need it."

"Me too, Jamie. Me too."

Then they split their paths. Edward Bowl watched Jamie sneaking across the large lawn from the back of the house. It seemed larger than he remembered. The rain intensified and the wind made an eerie sound. The darkness was palpable in the static air. He could almost feel it breathing on his face. He knew that Johnny Hawk was in that house.

Perhaps alive, perhaps not.

He checked the bulge in the back of his jeans to make sure he still had his gun, then walked as fast as he could along the perimeter, keeping his eyes on the windows. When he reached the kitchen, he paused and peeked inside, a hand flat on his forehead to reduce the glare. The utilities and the furniture looked dull in the darkness of the empty room. He made his way around the house until he was at the front, at the edge of the living room's cornered window. The house looked empty. The rain, pushed by the wind to an angle, tapped on the windows and the wooden siding of the house.

Could he have been wrong? Was it really possible that he had dragged Jamie into a complete nonsense operation? Giving him a gun, scaring the shit out of him? Or perhaps was it plausible that he led Johnny into the hands of a disturbed psychopath? Either way, he wasn't making very wise choices lately. Was it the grape-sized tumor growing in the middle of his brain? Maybe it was the size of a lemon by now? Or was it just that he had gone fucking crazy?

He gazed in the void, observing the invisible flow of his thoughts fighting one another, when a glimmer in the rain caught his attention. He squinted, trying to clear his vision, putting the glare in the grass in focus. When he saw the gleam again, he walked toward it and kneeled to grab it.

It was a wedding band.

The old heart that had hummed for almost sixty-five years

sank in his chest with the same violence of a cannonball shot into a bathtub. He turned the ring over to inspect it, putting in focus the engraved letters on the inside.

John and Ellen -- 06-05-2012

And that was when he heard the gunshot.

4

On the other side of the property, Jamie's heart was running so fast that, for a moment, he thought it would explode. It took him more than a few deep breaths to calm it down.

"How the fuck did I end up here?" he muttered as his eyes flashed back and forth between the windows of the house, as if he expected Wendy to see him at any moment. He felt the grip of the 9mm in his hands, rubbing his thumb on the safety lever Mr. Bowl had shown him, playing in his mind all the sequences of operations that led to shooting and maybe killing someone. He wondered if he would be able to do it quickly enough, if he would do it correctly at all. What would shooting someone feel like? What was the right amount of pressure to put on the trigger? Would he miss the target? Perhaps he was just going to be shot after all. His mind anchored to the hope that he wouldn't have to use that gun. Not now, not ever. Guns disgusted him. He had always thought of them as providers of a fake, too-easy sense of power.

He took a deep breath and moved to the side of the garage, where a rectangular window stood, hammered by the relentless rain. It was a few inches taller than he was. He tried to lift up on his toes, but that didn't get him a clear look into the garage. He found a vase, which had held pretty flowers once, now reduced to dried, lifeless stems. He flipped the vase over and hopped onto it. The window was now in his field of view. He wiped the outside of the glass with the sleeve of his jacket and peeked inside.

The glass was dusty but not obscured enough to hide the inside of the garage. Between the thick spider webs that filled the corners, the sight his eyes recorded was so shocking that he almost fell from the vase. The description of Wendy's white SUV that Mr. Bowl had given him became utterly irrelevant in a blink of an eye.

The chrome-plated details of the Jaguar XKE gleamed in the darkness of the room, like a lighthouse in a stormy, murky night. Jamie could clearly see that the keys were still in the ignition.

He jumped off the vase and ran with all the energy he had left back in the direction he came from, looking for Mr. Bowl.

Then he heard the gunshot.

It was so loud that it seemed it was coming from inside him, and he fell on his knees.

And the tears mixed with the warm rain.

5

The time is changing, Johnny thought. *It's slowing down*. Deep inside him, he knew he had been in the basement for less than a week, but it seemed like he had always lived there, like his life belonged there. And for how long had she been sitting there staring at him?

Whoever she was—definitely not the charming woman he had first made love to—she kept staring at him with a dreadful grin, not moving a muscle, as if she had frozen in the most unnatural expression she could create. The time had stretched, Johnny thought. In his utter desperation, time flowed at a different pace, but most importantly now, he really did not know how long she had been staring at him with that grin, and a two-barrel shotgun firmly in her hand.

She started to walk around the room, keeping her eyes on him. She moved jerkily, back and forth, making her look even more unnatural, if possible.

"Why don't you just do it?" Johnny asked in a trembling voice he had hoped to mask. Her dark eyes broadened into black holes and she looked surprised, as if she couldn't believe he had found the courage to talk. Then she hushed him, slowly bringing a pointer on her lips, fresh with crimson lipstick. She looked around the room, alternating from giggles that belonged to a kid, to hysterical laughter ending in a desperate whine.

He shivered. Witnessing that level of insanity was way

beyond what he had pictured in his mind. His leg began to shake helplessly, and there was nothing he could do to keep it under control. There was nothing he had under his control, besides his hopes that it would all end soon and with the least amount of pain possible. He looked at the shotgun and asked himself if she would use it now, or if she would opt for the taser again. The thought of it made him sick to his stomach. He retched, but only a few drops of acidic saliva came out. She looked at him and shook her head slowly as the insane grin re-emerged from the abyss.

Johnny realized, with a wave of unspeakable terror raging inside his chest, that Wendy—or whoever the hell she was right now—was having an episode of personality shift. He vaguely remembered Ellen explaining to him the mechanisms at play with patients that suffered from multiple personality disorder. Now he saw it happening in front of his eyes. States of mind alternated with one another, and Wendy's face passed through expressions filled with madness and sadness. Like an experienced actress, her features changed from the childish, to the grief, and ultimately back to evil. Johnny witnessed the dreadful metamorphosis like a gambler, waiting to see where the roulette's ball would stop.

The diary kept coming back to him. In a rare moment of lucidity she had handed it to him so he could save her. *Don't let her find it*, she had said with fear living in her eyes, as if she knew that losing the diary would mean losing herself forever.

"Remember that day?"

The voice came out way lower than he had hoped but still loud enough to catch her attention. The roulette of emotions stopped and she looked at him with disgust and incredulity. Her eyes widened again, so dark and deep that it seemed he was staring into a well with no end. Her cheeks, which had held a light rose blush a few days ago, were now hollowed. Her skin was pale and contrasted starkly with her freshly painted red lips. She had put the lipstick on in a rush, judging by the smears at the corners. Her mouth was a grimace of pain, wrath, and insanity.

"You remember that day, don't you, Wendy?" he said louder, fighting against the heat raging in his chest. "When you had butterflies in your stomach?"

She stiffened and stood up straight. Then, she grabbed the taser from her dress's front pocket and launched towards Johnny, sending electrons straight into his neck.

"*YOU FUCKING NOTHING, SHUT YOUR FUCKING MOUTH!*"

Then she dropped the stick on the floor, flinching at her own screams. Her lips were still wide open, but her eyes were scared. The current stopped flowing, but Johnny's limbs dropped lifelessly on the mattress. His head moved slowly when he regained consciousness.

She stared at him and began to hyperventilate. Something was happening. Another transformation? She could easily raise the rifle and smear his brain on the white concrete blocks behind him. Or she might have used the stick again, might have literally fried him to her pleasure until his heart stopped.

Instead, she dropped to her knees. Then she cried out, her screams mixed with whimpers. A hard fight began on the floor in front of him, but he couldn't watch. He forced himself to keep his eyes shut as the horror unfolded. The screams were nothing belonging to this world. The whines, on the contrary, belonged to a desperate prisoner trying to make her way out of an abyss of evil and darkness.

"I'm sorry for what happened to you," he screamed with all the strength he had left inside him. His eyes were still closed, and he felt tears flowing on his dry skin. "I'm sorry, Wendy. You deserved better than that. You deserved to be loved." And his last words were deafening in the silence that dropped suddenly in the room. There was not a sound, except for the rain that began to tap insistently outside.

He opened his eyes and saw her, standing right in front of him. She was Wendy again, exactly the way he had seen her before he got locked down and tortured one inch from death. Her eyes were filled with tears. But she wasn't looking at him. She stared straight ahead with her arm reaching toward the wall, her hand open and ready to be grabbed and held.

"You are so beautiful, Mom," she whispered, as tears rolled down her cheeks. She giggled, excited, and her other arm, the one holding the shotgun, raised. The holes in the barrels were looking straight into Johnny's eyes. He sobbed and lowered his head. No more pain. No more screams and horrors. *Hopefully there will be music*, he thought.

The shotgun fired like a thousand thunders.

6

Edward Bowl appeared from the corner, running toward Jamie. The young man kneeled on the wet grass. Edward reached him and seized him by the shoulders.

"The car, his car is in there," he stuttered. "Is... is he dead?"

"I don't know," Edward said shakily as he helped him up, and then they ran to the back door. The knob squeaked and they were in. The kitchen was dark and silent. Edward fished out the .44 from his jeans and cocked it.

"Stay behind me," he whispered to Jamie. He walked around the white marbled island. The basement's door was open, and a weak light came out of it. Edward led the way down with both hands solidly wrapped around the gun. A terrible smell reached his nostrils, and it got worse with every step.

The sight of what came next would haunt him for the remainder of his life. His arms relaxed and he put the gun down as he realized it wasn't necessary anymore.

7

Copper City's law enforcement squad—which consisted of Sheriff River, the two deputies Cecilia Starr and Buck Robertson, aka Buckie, and the night-knocker Pete Sullivan—

housed its headquarters on Main Street, in a squat building with fake red brick siding. The precinct was a modest open space with two desks, one bigger than the other. A ten-by-ten cage with rusted bars had been placed in the far-right corner, and the filthy mattress that was laid in it had been used most often by Ross Ferris, usually after a Friday night drunk fight at the El Dorado. On the other side of the room, against the wall, stood a table with a coffee maker and a basket full of candies: the break area.

The only room with walls and a door in the whole building was the interrogation room.

Allen River was a fat man with deep blue eyes, whereas Buckie was a tall, skinny fella with tiny dark eyes and bulging front teeth. They both sat at one end of a steel table, which held Joe to-go cups of steaming coffee.

"So, let me check that I get this completely straight, Edward," River said, putting on what he clearly thought was a smart detective face, as he read through his notes. "Your friend with the fancy car disappears, and initially you think he just hit the road, but then you don't believe that no more, and you go look for him in the Jags' house because he was banging the doc's hot daughter. And then you hear a gunshot. So you get in the house and then down to the basement and..." He paused, gesturing with his right hand to invite him to continue.

Edward Bowl took a sip of coffee and grimaced at the taste of it. He closed his eyes, to mentally recall the scene he was desperately trying to remove from his mind, and he was back in that basement.

The smell was horrible; the kind of smell that comes out of a bucket that has stored shit and piss for a few days. He saw the man's body first. Johnny Hawk lay on his left side. His ankle was chained to the wall, and there were burns on his whole body. He had been tortured. The man's face was a triumph of blood. Edward Bowl rushed towards him and kneeled to check his pulse. Weak, but life was still pumping into him.

"Call 911. Ambulance and firefighters," he said, turning to Jamie. He stood on the stairs with both hands on his head. And as Mr. Bowl turned, he saw the gleam of the shotgun's barrels, smoke still coming out of it, lying near what was left of Wendy Jag's head. His first thought was: *Just like her dad.*

Just like her dad, she had pulled that same trigger. Just like him, she had come to realize that was the only way out of the darkness. And just like it happened to her father, she had found that moment to free herself, blowing her brain out and shattering a piece of skull onto the walls and ceiling. It never had been only about taking their own lives; it was about erasing those awful grins, reaching the bottom of the endless wells that lived in their eyes.

The remains of a beautiful young woman lay in front of his eyes, her arm jutting in a tiny rectangle of light on the slate.

8

The waiting room of the County Hospital was strangely quiet at night. Edward Bowl was sitting between the Emergency Room entrance and the Traumatic Injuries ward. In his experience he had seen that the world was full of people getting hurt every day. It didn't matter if it was the Walter Reed Memorial or the ER of a god-forgotten town in the middle of rural New Mexico.

The double door kept opening and closing as the head nurse passed in and out relentlessly. She wore a lavender uniform. Edward gazed to his right and saw Jamie. His eyes were closed and his hood was up. It might have seemed he was taking a nap if it wasn't for his foot nervously tapping on the floor. Edward felt sorry for him, a young man escaped from his own hell only to jump into a brand new one. What he had seen in that basement would haunt him for endless nights.

Twenty minutes later, a tall fit man in his forties appeared in the waiting room, an unflinching expression painted on his face. He might have been able to give the best and worst news without even blinking. Edward stood as the doctor approached, while Jamie kept his seat, his tremors increasing.

"How is he?" Edward went first.

"We moved him to the ICU. His lungs collapsed and we had to intubate him. He is currently sedated," the doctor answered in a far warmer tone than his features had led Edward to expect. He cleared his throat, forewarning that he wasn't done with the news. "An infection has developed from his flank, which suffered third degree burns. Seven teeth have been extracted from his mouth."

"Is he in danger?" Jamie asked.

"No, he is not." The doctor turned to him calmly. "The early signs are encouraging, but we should wait and see how the night goes. In the meantime, I strongly recommend you go have a restful night. Your friend is in a safe place now."

They left the hospital and drove back home. Mr. Bowl called Greg Bollard and briefed him about Johnny's condition. He was on his way back to New Mexico.

The sky was clear, moonless and full of stars. Half of them might be dead, Jamie thought. They might have died a million years ago or yesterday, and we wouldn't know the difference. These nuclear reactors, burning their life out and still showing up as tiny dots in an endless sea of darkness.

When Mr. Bowl finally went to bed, Jamie lit up a Marlboro and threw the empty pack in the crackling fire. He drew the diary out of his pocket. He got goosebumps when his fingers passed over the engravings on the leather cover, and he remembered how stealthily he had put the diary in his pocket before the cops could. It had stuck out, half covered, from the bottom of the filthy mattress where Johnny's tortured body lay. He had taken it without thinking. It had been impossible to resist. Part of him knew that something important was in those pages, like in every page there was a story to be told.

Now, he flicked through the pages without reading them.

His thumb stopped on one with a fold in it. And so he read it, holding his breath, utterly unaware that was the page that had saved Johnny Hawk's life.

9

September 19th , 1995

Dear diary,

I'm not completely sure about it, but I think I might have just had the best day of my life. I think, or was it maybe the worst? One day I asked Mrs. Gable how would I know when I'm happy? How do I know when I'm sad? Because it all feels the same. I remember she looked at me in a funny way and she said: "It's different with everyone. When it happens to me, I feel it in my stomach. Like butterflies are flying into it." I never quite understood what she meant.

Until now. I think I know what she meant because I feel them, the butterflies.

Daddy called me from the basement and I knew right away what he wanted. It is almost every week now. He always wants that when he calls me down in the basement, with that fake voice. He wore that creepy mask and the white gown. He still thinks I don't know but I do. I do know it's him. It's not the Tooth Fairy. To be honest I really believed it was, the first time, but the second time I recognized the smell of whiskey. It was the same bottle on top of the fridge, the one Daddy drinks. And also, the calls were happening often, even when I didn't lose any tooth.

But I kept pretending, diary. You see, it started to happen after Mom died. So I pretended I didn't know. Because everything was already too much. It's been a long time since I started pretending not knowing.

When he called me down this evening, with his fake female voice, everything felt like all the other times. I didn't want to but I never refused. I brought Ben with me, like I always do. It helps to have it there with me. I sat on the chair, and I looked up at the girl on the swing beneath the stars. I remember the day he drew it for me. That was my safe place in the worst moments. When he finished, he sat at his desk, like he always did and I would normally go back up at that point. But he didn't tell me to. He grabbed a plastic bag from the drawer. The bag had some crystals in it. He dropped some and crushed them on the table.

He must have been already out of himself because he took the mask off when I was still on the chair. Even though I knew that it was him, it was still shocking to see it had been him all that time. It hurt to see how consumed he was. I had never seen him so unhappy. He breathed the crystals in his nose. His eyes were red as the devil and his face was sweet and pale, consumed by the pain. He passed out, face on the desk.

I looked at him for a long time. I didn't know what to do. I didn't know how I felt. Normally I would be worried, but I wasn't and that was confusing. A feeling had started in my stomach but I didn't know what it was. Something was happening and I felt lighter, like a weight had been slowly taken off me. And I sat there looking at this man, snoring in his own drool after forcing his daughter to take her panties down in the basement, pretending to be the Tooth Fairy.

And the more I processed how pathetic he looked, the more that feeling grew inside me until the point I couldn't ignore it anymore. At that moment I knew exactly what I had to do. And so I did, my dear diary. It was so loud down there that I can still feel it in my ears. I stood near him for a few minutes and I watched his hand becoming cold and wan. I went upstairs and showered, and then I called the police and waited for them on the stairs. I had to put up the shocked girl expression on my face, but it wasn't that bad honestly. I've gotten really good at pretending.

Deep down inside me I had finally discovered what happiness felt like.

I had butterflies in my stomach.

ABOUT THE AUTHOR

Davide Tarsitano is an author of novels and short stories.

He was born in Italy in 1989. He was raised in Cosenza, a small town in the south, and educated in its public schools. He eventually found his way to University of Calabria and to University of Modena and Reggio Emilia where he graduated, respectively, in Mechanical Engineering B.S. and Automotive Engineering M.S. He currently works in the race car industry in North America.

Meanwhile, at the age of seven, he found the passion of his life when his dad bought him a book from the Goosebumps series by R.L Stine named *Night of the Living Dummy*. This escalated quickly, inevitably leading him to Edgar Allan Poe, H.P. Lovecraft and Stephen King.

By the time he was fourteen, he had written short stories

and a full screenplay of a horror movie, never produced.

In the following years his interest broadened towards cosmic horror, science fiction and dystopian fiction.

He met his wife in 2016 and married her in 2019.

In 2018 he started to write his first horror novel: *The Tooth Fairy*, which represents his debut as an author.

For more information, please visit:

dtarsitano.com

Or connect with him on social media:

facebook.com/davidetarsitanoauthor
instagram.com/dtarsitanoofficial
twitter.com/DtarsitanoO

5/23

Made in United States
North Haven, CT
16 April 2023

35506832R00167